"Gil Brewer's Florida is not and steamy and maddening. His books almost always have a man on the run, missing loot, and a scorching lustful heat that fills the air. … Brewer fills it with enough excitement and action that it reels you in."
—Dave Wilde

"Typical Brewer. Dames, death, crime, and mystery."
—*GoodReads*

"The plot feels a bit like Brewer was flying by the seat of his pants as Lee runs around trying to figure out how a bank robbery is connected to a missing husband and a hacked up corpse."
—Kurt Reichenbaugh

"Permeated with sweaty desperation."
—James Reasoner, *Rough Edges*

WILD
by Gil Brewer

Black Gat Books • Eureka California

WILD

Published by Black Gat Books
A division of Stark House Press
1315 H Street
Eureka, CA 95501, USA
griffinskye3@sbcglobal.net
www.starkhousepress.com

ISBN: 979-8-88601-109-8

Text design by Mark Shepard, shepgraphics.com
Cover design by Jeff Vorzimmer, ¡caliente!design, Austin, Texas
Cover art by Harry Barton

First Stark House Press/Black Gat Edition: August 2024

ONE

She sat there on the couch and watched me; a sweet, slim, sexy number wearing a white nylon dress and white pumps. Thick auburn hair framed an oval face that faintly hinted of Oriental ancestry, a face I would never forget. She was a year or two younger than I. She stared at me steadily through minutely slanted, tragic dark blue eyes.

Memory had fired old emotions the moment I saw her. She felt it, too, but we both avoided the words. There was the interim before the war, then the war years, and ten years away from the home town, between now and the intense time we'd spent together back in high school. She was the dream you remember in the occasional long dark night when the span of years between then and now is empty of everything but painful regret.

She had called me. I had come to her. Her name was changed, now. She was changed. More lovely in every way.

"I'm in trouble," she said.

"Tell me about it."

I listened and remembered.

The world may be harsh and blood-filled; a cynical street, your street. But you're just a bowl of mush when you remember.

The dark corner of spring. Elms in the wind, dashing warm rain across streetlights.

The first kiss at that party, in somebody's home. It

was in the bedroom, with coats and hats piled on the bed; the smells of wool and felt and fur and perfume. She had asked me to help her find her purse.

The way she stirred when I touched her. How it would be forever.

Stardust. That was "our" song.

Once in a While. That Old Feeling. I Can't Get Started. Indian Summer....

The taste of her lips. The way she looked at me.

A thousand torments.

It's still there. It always will be there. Only you can't have it, because contradictorily it's gone forever, too.

I listened to her. Finally she stopped talking.

I said, "You've tried to reason with him?"

"I phoned him several times. At first he cursed me. Really bad — worse than I can say. The past few times I called, he won't answer the phone."

"Why don't you just go home yourself, then?"

"I told you — Lee." She hesitated. "I nearly called you Mr. Baron. Silly, isn't it?"

"Yeah."

"I'm afraid to go home," she said. "That's why I need your help. The afternoon he caught me with — with the person I told you about, I thought he was going to kill me, he was so mad. I just got away in time. He even chased the car when I drove off. He was like a maniac." Her eyes were worried. "You're a stranger to him. If you'll just talk to him, I feel you could smooth him down."

"Does he carry a gun?"

"My husband?" She seemed surprised. "No."

"What was this other 'person's' name?"

"I'd rather keep him out of this."

"Just one of those things?"

"Yes. It's all over. It was never really anything. I was bored and unhappy. I'm sorry for what I did. Carl caught us kissing. He's made much too much of it."

"Carl is your husband?"

"Yes." Her expression became earnest. "Will you please help me, Lee?"

I turned and looked out the door of her duplex apartment at the Southern Pines Motel. Rain brightly iced the Florida skies, lanced green palms. My car was across the street, parked in a deep puddle.

"I'll have to know a few things," I said.

Her voice was low. "I'll tell you anything I can."

I went over and sat in a chair directly in front of the couch.

"When did all this happen, Ivor?" Unlike the way she had nearly used my last name, I could never call her Mrs. Hendrix. Her maiden name had been Heira. "Yesterday?"

"No. Over a month ago."

I digested that for a moment. She was deeply troubled. She spoke melodically, with carefully broad A's. Southern-born, she had obviously been further schooled in the North, after I'd known her, maybe at Smith. It was somehow a strange mixture. She had large breasts and she aimed them at you when she talked.

"How did you happen to call me?" I said. "I've only been in town six days. I'm not even open for business yet."

Her eyes widened. "But I thought — your agency

was advertised in the classified section of the newspaper." She nudged her lower lip with even white teeth. "I wanted someone experienced in dealing with people. I felt that in your business, you'd know how to handle a thing like this." She hesitated. "I do have a little confession to make, Lee. The ad was under your father's name, James Baron. I didn't know you worked with him till I talked to you."

"I never did work with him," I said. "He died recently. I've taken over the business."

"I'm sorry." She was no longer eager. "Perhaps this isn't in your line."

"Now you're doubtful," I said. "As for qualifications, I'm a licensed private investigator, Ivor. Both here and in California. I guess I'll be here from now on. I was a year with the Mallory and Kartel agency in San Francisco. Before that I was a cop on the force in Chicago. Previously, I pulled several years in Europe with Army Intelligence. Would you care to see credentials?" I grinned at her.

"Oh, no — that's all right."

She crossed her legs. She was the type girl who would always have difficulties when it came to crossing legs. Rebellious skirts. The gesture would brighten dark moments with revelations of plump assets that make the heart beat hard.

"Shall we continue?" I said. "Or would you rather call in somebody else? I can recommend...."

"I want *you*, Lee."

I made no comment. I felt faintly stiff with her, as if there were a wispy barrier of time that neither of us could quite break through. She had colored faintly.

Very, very lovely. She smiled a faintly embarrassed smile. I wondered if she recalled saying those same words to me long years ago, with a different meaning. The smile made her still lovelier.

"Anything you tell me is strictly between us, Ivor. In case that's bothering you. Now, can you tell me why you want to return to your husband, after all this?"

She hesitated. "I do want to be truthful," she said.

"It's best."

"I'm just not sure how I feel about Carl. I don't know for sure whether I *could* stick it out with him again, now that all this has happened." She paused, the eyes very serious. "I do know I can't just leave him — without clearing things up between us."

I said nothing.

"We hadn't been getting along too well," she said. "But a lot of that was my fault."

"A month's a long time on a thing like this. It may be just a question of pride. You won't go to him, he won't come to you. He's probably chewing his nails now, wishing he'd never said anything, hoping you'll come home. He'd be a fool to think anything else."

"I'm afraid it's not like that at all."

"You've been staying here for a month?"

"No. I came back to town five days ago. I've been trying to work up courage. Then I had this idea."

"Where were you?"

"At Carl's aunt's. In Orlando."

"Not with this other — person?"

"No. I thought if I went away, then got in touch with Carl, didn't let him know where I was — but it didn't work."

"The other guy's no problem?"

"No."

"What is the aunt's name?"

She began to chill. "Haskins. Elizabeth Haskins."

"She didn't get in touch with your husband?"

"Absolutely no." She took a deep breath, uncrossed her legs, and crossed them the other way. There were soft warm silken sounds in the room. She clasped her hands around her knee, watching me. "I just want you to see Carl," she said. "Act as a sort of intermediary. That's all."

"Suppose he won't intermediate?"

"Well — " Again she colored briefly. "I've considered that, too. I thought perhaps you could throw a scare into him — tell him I'm desperate, that I might harm myself. That's up to you, of course."

"I see."

"That wouldn't be too much trouble, would it?"

"You think it'll work?"

"I'm hoping."

"He won't listen to you at all?"

She shook her head. "When he gets mad, it's awful. He said he'd kill me, if he caught me."

"Yet you want to go back to him."

She turned her gaze downward, then looked up at me and half-smiled. "I just don't know," she said. "I've got to talk with him, Lee."

"It's a little out of my line. Who should I tell him I am? Any particular story you want cooked up?"

"No. Tell him the truth."

It had been a loaded question.

"What about the 'desperate' part?"

"I *am* desperate."

"Your family still in town?"

She hesitated, tugged her skirt over her knee, let it slide back under her thumb. "Mother and Dad are both gone, Lee. My sister, Asa, still lives here. *She's* married now. You didn't know him. Elk Crafford." She thought a moment. "Asa and I don't get along."

"Everything helps the picture."

"Oh," she said coldly.

"Don't get me wrong. It's better if I know certain things."

"I'm sorry. Will you do it for me?"

"I'll have a try. I won't promise anything. What is your husband's work?"

"He isn't doing anything just now. He and Elk — but that's not pertinent, really."

"Where do you live?"

"In a trailer." There was a shade of bitterness in her tone. "Out in Pine Park. You know where Pine Park is?"

I watched her. "It was a swell place to park and neck, when I was in high school. If I remember right. I suppose it's changed."

She looked at the backs of her hands.

I stood up. I didn't want to leave. "I guess that's it for now."

She rose from the couch and looked at me with those eyes. There was the thick auburn hair, and the fine body under the tightly smooth white nylon dress. We were close for the moment and there was perfume, too — so faint and elusive you might go crazy trying to find it again.

"Is fifty dollars enough? I'm afraid I can't afford more. I know this sort of thing is expensive."

I felt the blood in my shoulders and head. "You're my first client since I've come home," I said. "It's an offbeat thing. I'm not sure I can help you. Let's just make it a favor, okay?"

I heard myself say that, marveling.

"I'm sorry," she said. "I insist you take the money, Lee. I wouldn't feel right unless you did." She turned, stepped over beside the couch, and leaned down in that wonderful way they have of leaning down, and brought up a white cylindrical purse. She unsnapped it, reached in, and handed me a fifty dollar bill.

I looked at it and put it in my pocket.

"I'm terribly impatient, Lee. I'll be hanging on strings till you let me know."

She held out her hand. I took it. It was very smooth and soft and cool. Time sprawled headlong back across rocky years. I wanted to say something deeply nostalgic. I said, "You're sure he'll be out there? If he's not, what would you like me to do?"

Her face did not change expression and there was the gentle pressure of her fingers.

"He should be there," she said. "If he's not, the key's on a ledge under the step. You can go inside and wait for him. He never stays away long. I mean, if you would?"

"Well, I wouldn't do that."

"I want you to, Lee. It's my home. You have my permission."

I held her hand a moment longer, until she turned deftly and opened the door. I went outside. It was still raining and there was something of long-lost summers in the air.

I shrugged into my wet slicker and started down the walk toward the street.

I spotted a telephone booth on the next corner, stopped the car, and called the *Journal*. I canceled the agency ad James Baron had kept running in the classified for years. Then I flopped the phone directory up on the shelf again and checked. The Hendrix number was listed under Carl's name. I dialed and waited.

It rang a few times.

Somebody picked up the phone on the other end, breathing fast and nervous, then quieting.

"Ivor?" a man said. "Ivor — that you?"

"Telephone company," I said. "Testing. Line down out here. Would you hang up, please?"

He hung up.

TWO

A fat man wearing mud-splashed overalls was probing beside the road with a crowbar. A drainage ditch was plugged. He looked up, round and red-faced, as I stopped the car and walked over.

I mentioned her name and asked about Pine Park.

"Hendrix?" he said between spits. Sunburned eyebrows suddenly shot up. "Oh, sho, now, I reckon you mean *them*. Lives out in that 'ere trailer. Foller the road an' keep a-goin'. Cain't miss hit." He shifted the crowbar, tossed an amber stream of tobacco juice at a puddle, and struck dead center. He dug me in the ribs with a frayed elbow and said, "Heh, heh, heh."

I thanked him and went back to the car. The rain was pale fizz. Over to the right the sky was a pink-gray tent above the city. Out there the sky was gray-black. I drove past a flooded intersection on the dirt road.

I saw the trailer. The road descended in a gentle slope past a wooded section, then curved around the bite of a small lake. Across the lake, the trailer crouched like a battered packing crate on cement blocks. A tired old car leaned beside it. A rutted drive wound from the main road to the trailer. The land was fingered with dripping slash pine, cypress, oak, and scrub.

Rather than chance getting mired, I parked on the road shoulder and walked through soft earth along the drive.

The air smelled faintly as if someone had just finished cooking sour cabbage.

I headed for the trailer. Electric light wires looped from tree to tree, with smashed bulbs hanging on them. The ground around the trailer was littered with junk: half-eaten sandwiches, beer bottles, whisky bottles, gin bottles, chicken feathers, a torn red corduroy skirt, an empty caviar tin, a burnt mattress, one black spike-heeled pump curled inward upon itself like a scorpion that had committed suicide.

I tried the trailer door. It was locked.

The car was an ancient-vintage Hudson, rusting in a heap, tires flat. Beyond the trailer was the last weedy vestige of what had once been a garden, surrounded by cement blocks. Beyond that, where the pine woods thickened, I saw a square, unpainted cement block house about the size of a small garage. High in the dirty sky, a buzzard wheeled mistily.

I kicked the trailer door. It didn't rattle. Windows were opaque with dust, shielded on the inside with Venetian blinds.

I walked around the trailer, kicking tin cans. A blackened pit in the earth showed where they burned trash. Half-burned newspapers; hunks of wood; an old crate; tin cans, bottles; wet cardboard cartons; a large old leather suitcase with heavy straps and buckles, initialed "K. S. — " something-or-other and pretty well singed; what looked like smashed parts of a dressing table. Everything was stirred together and soaking wet.

I looked toward the denser woods, the cement block structure. There was a worn, mud-packed path. I took it.

Closer, I saw the heavy, iron-hinged, cross-strapped wooden door. A brass padlock hung on the hasp, but the lock was open. The smell of sour cabbage struck me again, stronger now.

The door was cracked partially open, rain brightly flickering against gray wood. I booted the door sharply with my heel and looked inside.

The odor was no longer polite.

I held a handkerchief over my nose and mouth and stepped through, pushing the door wide. A dusty window high on the back wall shed dim light across the body.

He resembled a partially unwrapped mummy.

Both arms were gone, and somebody had done a hatchet job on his face.

I began to feel at home in Florida.

THREE

I looked at the stilled stage of death. There was that greater silence, more than an empty room, more felt than seen.

One room. Hard-packed dirt floor. Doorless closet with sink and toilet. Gently sloped unpainted raftered ceiling. An old steel cot with a bent leg, covered with two worn Army blankets. Several raddled adventure and crime magazines strewn on the floor, looking as if they had been gnawed by rats.

And the dead man.

A length of grease-blackened tow-chain was slung through a steel ring fastened to a steel plate in the wall. The chain was wrapped around the dead man's waist and ankles. It was padlocked to prevent slippage.

Afternoon shadows began to darken.

A car's engine revved. I turned in time to see a maroon Olds sedan move past on the dirt road by the lake. A pale, blunt man's face flashed in the driver's window, staring. It was too far away, too shadowed to tell anything else. The sound of the car died with distance.

I moved over to the dead man. What was left of a heavy growth of beard covered his face. He wore blue, frayed trousers, and once-white tennis shoes with no socks. He wore no shirt or undershirt. His ribs were badly caved, stomach a hungry cavity. He looked starved.

There were two padlocks on the chains. I saw no key.

A corpse looks strange without arms.

A straight-backed chair was turned on its side. A large wad of rolled cloth lay in the corner by the cot. It was a blue suit, damp and mud-caked around the trouser cuffs. Pockets revealed half a comb, lint and tobacco crumbs, an empty package of mentholated cigarettes. The trouser cuffs held a single paper clip. The suit had been purchased at a men's clothing store in Tampa.

I remembered Chief of Homicide Lowell Haddock, and how he would like things. I rolled the suit up again, dropped it on the floor, and stared at it. I put my handkerchief away, and stepped into the small closet. The sink was dirty.

Back beside the dead man, I knelt and went through his pockets. Fat brown wallet, very worn. Folded piece of notepaper. Four toothpicks. Dime, nickel, and two pennies.

I took the wallet and paper to the door, and held them in diminishing afternoon light. The paper unfolded limply, revealing a penciled scrawl:

"Carl, honey — If you wake before I return. I went to the A & P for some groceries. Please, will you call Elk and ask him again? He's just got to give you some money. Cold sherry in frige. I won't be long — Ivor."

I looked down at the dead man, then refolded the paper and had a look at the wallet.

Identification card, driver's license, a wad of unpaid

bills in Carl Hendrix's name. There were a number of cards from paint supply stores, used car lots, real estate brokers. Twelve dollars in limp singles. Two snapshots of Ivor. One was recent, posed on the beach. She wore a skimpy, two-piece black swimsuit, revealing a happy smile, windy hair, and a lush, beautiful body. The other photo was a head and shoulders; self-conscious, startled high-schoolish expression. It was an old photo and she had changed. But I remembered that look maybe too well.

I put everything back into the wallet, then returned the folded note and wallet to the dead man's pockets as I'd found them.

I started to turn away, then knelt by the body again. In stuffing the wallet back into the hip pocket, I had moved the body slightly to one side. The surface of the earthen floor in the room was packed nearly to the hardness of cement, except where the body had been lying. I touched the earth. It was loose, and a colored piece of paper winked. Hendrix's body had been lying on it. I scraped loose soil away, pulled out a narrow broken paper band. There was type printing on the paper, and beneath the print, a paler-inked stamp. The band had once secured together ten one hundred dollar bills. The pale-inked stamp read: UNION TRUST — LAKETOWN, FLORIDA.

A robbery had occurred about a month ago in the Union Trust Bank, at Laketown. I had followed the newspaper stories. Close to four hundred thousand dollars had been taken. The money had been from Florida citrus groves, being held in transit at Laketown for a matter of five hours. The men pulling the robbery had escaped.

I stared at the paper band. Then I put it back where I'd found it and pulled the body in position over the loosened earth again.

Enigmatic, to say the least.

Outside the cement block house, I locked the padlock on the hasp after closing the door. It still rained softly as I walked around the cement house. The steel ring was fastened through the cement to a circular plate, locked with a rusted nut outside.

I returned to the trailer and checked around under the door step for the key she had mentioned. It wasn't there.

Balancing on the cement block doorstep, I lifted my foot and slammed my heel against the door, close to the lock. The door snapped, but didn't open. Something flipped off the top ledge and rang against the block, twinkling into the mud beside the handle of an old stubby broom.

It was the key. I leaned down to pick it up.

I heard flying feet. It was too late to act, to even see. I turned my head straight into the savage rush of feet and fur and snarling teeth. It struck me, growling deep-throated, snapping snarls. I sprawled back into the mud, trying to cover my face.

It was a dog, an enormous hound, slimy with mud and rain. On my back, it pinned me down. The jaws yawned viciously for my throat. I caught both hands into the grimed fur and slung it with the wild strength of fright. I heard it land, scrabbling, emitting savage snaps and growls.

I came part way to my feet and sprang for the broom

handle, caught the handle in one fist and gouged for the key shining against the ground.

Again the hound leaped. It soared. I slammed at it with the broom, on my feet, backing for the trailer door.

Again the hound rushed, a monstrous bundle of rain-soaked fur and fangs.

"Back!"

I was on the cement block doorstep. The broom struck the hound in the chest. The animal flipped backward, landed on its side, was immediately on its feet, forelegs spread, head down, eyes up, jaws open, the long fangs bared beneath the tightly drawn snout.

I fumbled with the key, trying to get it in the lock, working with one hand behind and to my side. I got the key in the lock and turned it. The door gave.

Again the hound flew at me.

I slung the broom at the beast and leaped back against the door. It sprang inward. I got inside the trailer, saw the hound flying at me again, and slammed the door closed. The dog crashed thunderously against the closed door. A dish fell somewhere and broke. The door held.

I stood there, gasping. I was soaked with sweat.

The hound was outside the door, growling like a low-toned motor.

I peeled off my rain slicker, dropped it on the floor, took out my handkerchief and mopped my face, head, and neck.

There was a bottle of Old Overholt standing in a drainboard by a small sink. I found a clean glass, poured it half full, watching my hands shake, and drank the good rye whisky. I refilled the glass to a third and drank that, looking around the trailer.

There was a large, rumpled bunk at the rear, covered with a pale blue blanket and pink sheets. A large horizontal window was over the bunk. I opened the blinds on the windows, and pale light slipped inside to keep me company.

The hound continued to growl and pant outside.

Along the wall opposite the door was a stove, sink, the drainboard, and cupboards all paneled in natural wood. Under the drainboard was a small refrigerator. The floor was white-and-black checked linoleum, covered by the bunk with a blue rug. There was a double-doored closet on the other side, by the bunk. To the front, at the hitch-end, was a dining nook. Beside the entrance was a small oil stove. There had once been a partition between the living and sleeping area, but it had been torn out.

I poured another slug of the whisky and drank it. I put a dollar bill on the drainboard, set the bottle on it.

Then I searched the trailer.

There were three clean dresses in the closet, faint with her perfume. I pictured the tragic eyes. An unopened bottle of Gordon's Gin lay at the bottom of the closet among old shoes and a wadded roll of nylon stockings. Some men's sports shirts hung beside the dresses, two pairs of slacks, and a worn brown suit with empty pockets. I shoved the clothes aside and a broad slab of veneer at the side of the closet rattled loosely. I touched it and it fell to the floor. It had worked something like a sliding panel. Three letters in envelopes nestled against a two-by-four. They were addressed to Carl Hendrix.

The letters were from an address at Grove Point, over on Tampa Bay, the other side of town. They were from Asa Crafford. They smelled sexy, and I remembered Asa sharply. Apparently, she hadn't changed much, only expanded in experience. They were the hottest letters I'd ever read, and I had seen some blast-furnace love epistles in my time. These reached an ultimate. They seethed, boiled and fumed. Every word was a wet hot caress. Blatantly orgiastic, she went into minute detail about their love calisthenics, with wanton examples for a hopeful next meeting.

There might have been some humor in it, if a dead man wasn't lying out there in extremely bad shape, even for a dead man.

Asa Crafford. Ivor Hendrix's sister.

On each letter was penned a notation: *"Please burn this."*

Why do they write them if they want them burned?

Maybe he imagined they would turn to ashes of their own volition. They did have plenty of volition. Maybe he'd planned to sell them over on First Street. They would've brought a high price.

He'd made a mistake, keeping them. Or had he?

I checked postmarks. They were mailed about a month before, received during the first few days Ivor Hendrix had been away. According to their contents, Asa and Carl had been at it for a time, though.

I put the letters back, fixed the veneer, then checked the trailer window by the door. The hound was gone. I'd forgotten to explain to him that I liked dogs.

The telephone was under the table in the dining nook. I got it up on the table, went around and sat on the bench, and called police headquarters.

I asked for Lowell Haddock and waited a moment, then hung up quickly. I closed my eyes and rubbed them with thumb and forefinger, then dialed Information and asked for the number of the Southern Pines Motel. In a moment I had Ivor on the line.

I told her who I was and explained that I wanted to talk with her, that I'd see her as soon as possible. "Appreciate it if you didn't leave your apartment. Just wait there for me."

"Did you see Carl?"

"Yes."

"How did he act?" She was worried.

"Quite calm."

"Well — what did he have to say?"

"Nothing much, really."

"Is he going to be sensible about this?"

"Very. Listen, I can't talk now." I hesitated, wanting to ask her a hundred pointed questions. I gnawed the inside of my cheek, feeling like a louse. "Look," I said. "If you'll ..."

She broke in. "Will he let me come back?"

"Ivor. I've got to hang up. I'll be around by your place as soon as I can get there."

Trouble again. "Please."

"Just wait for me. Got that?"

I hung up, looked over at the bottle of Old Overholt, then dialed police headquarters again and asked the same voice for Lowell Haddock. He finally came on. I told him I had found a man's body and pictured

Haddock in my mind's eyes, hunched at his desk in front of the rain-streaked alley window, scrubbing his sparse, sweating gray head, his chunky red face set in very stern lines. I had met him and talked with him three times, previously. James Baron had told me a lot about him.

"Who is this?" Haddock said.

I told him who I was.

"How did you happen on this, Lee?"

"Routine investigation for a client."

He let that hang there for a time.

"Who's the client, Lee?"

"I can't say at this time. I won't hold anything back, Lowell. I just want a chance to speak with my client first. I'll be in touch with you."

He didn't push it. "Who's the dead guy?"

"The name is Carl Hendrix."

He said dryly, "There anything else you'd like to tell me, Lee?"

I hesitated. He was on top and knew it. My nose began to ache across the bridge. It was stupid to try and hold things back from the police. On the other hand, in this instance, it could be stupid not to do what you thought was right, even if somebody else thought it wrong. If I fouled up, that was no good, either. But if this killing had something to do with the Laketown robbery, and I managed to get a lead, it could mean good things. Telling Haddock about the paper currency band I'd found might stall me and tip them to something. They would find it soon enough.

"I guess there's nothing else, Lowell."

Haddock made a sound like a fly buzzing into a bird

bath. This was ticklish business. I didn't want either him or Chief of Police Howard Garlik forming snap opinions of me right now. James Baron had played ball too hard with all of them. I didn't want them getting the idea I would take their orders and tear up my ticket, just because they nodded their old gray heads.

I felt as if I were being watched. It was a creepy feeling. The rain fell heavier on the trailer roof now, and outside it seemed remote and dark.

"Lee, you do me a big favor and wait right there. I'd like to have a chat with you. Old Jim and I were close friends. I always knew when you finally came home, you'd be made of the same fine stuff."

"Come down out of the palm tree, Lowell. I've been knocking around in this business for a long time, remember?"

His tone changed. "What, son?"

"Forget it."

"Now, look, son — "

"Go ahead. Keep on calling me that."

"Jim and I were very close, Lee."

I lowered my voice and spoke carefully. "Good-by."

I hung up, feeling touchy about the phone call. I had wanted things to go right. The Florida Gulf Coast held big promise.

The feeling that I was being watched made my ears itch. I looked around, then stood up fast.

A man stared at me through the window over the bunk at the rear of the trailer. His features were faint.

I moved fast around the table, headed for the door. The face vanished. Feet scrambled. I heard savage animal-like running and panting.

That hound.

The door snapped open.

"Don't move."

He stared at me over the double barrel of a shotgun. A big guy, soaking wet, with black hair hanging over his forehead.

I watched him without speaking.

"I mean it," he said nervously. "You move and I'll shoot."

He shouldered inside and closed the door. Something smashed resoundingly against the door, clawing and growling. He opened the door. The hound flopped wetly in across the linoleum, whined softly, cocked his head at me, then shook himself. Water sprayed from floor to ceiling.

"Who the hell are you?" the man said.

FOUR

The hound shook himself good and dry. He took his time. I moved my hand to wipe some of the fragrant spray off my face.

"Don't," the guy said.

His eyes flickered curiously with the look they get when they're nervous and haven't much control. He was young, in his early twenties. He wore a heavy black raincoat, gleaming wetly. His gaze steadied, and he frowned.

"How long we going to stand here?" I said quietly.

"Till you explain to me who you are and what you're

doing here."

The shotgun was steady. He reached back, pawed around, then laid his hand on the wall switch. He knew right where it was. A bright overhead light came on.

I said, "I might ask you the same thing."

He coughed lightly, watching me under sparse black brows that looked like black watercolor paint. His face was waxen, without color. The lips were pale.

The hound panted and squeaked and dripped.

"You broke in," he said.

"If that's what you call opening the door with a key."

"Don't get funny."

He meant it. He didn't like people to get funny. The shotgun lifted brightly and he shuffled two inches toward me.

"Where is she?" he said.

"Move the gun," I said. "I'll be as nervous as you in a minute. Something might happen. Move the gun."

"Where is she?" he said again.

"Let's have a name."

The hound showed me his teeth. About four feet separated me from the end of the shotgun. I took a step backward.

He moved forward. "I told you not to move."

The shotgun barrel dipped.

I went for him hard and mad. I smashed the barrel to the left, wrapped my hand around it. The barrel swung up. The gun blasted straight through the roof. The guy yelled. The dog leaped, barking.

We both held ends of the shotgun. I got a shoulder underneath and came back hard. The gun broke loose.

I heaved it at the sink, wheeled and plowed into him with everything I had.

He grunted as I whipped my fist into his gut, against the black slicker.

We sprawled toward the door. The guy got his hand on the doorknob, holding it. The door swung open, with the hound snapping and snarling around our feet. I twisted and slung the guy against the sink as the dog flew at me. I ducked aside, and the dog flew right on out the door. I slammed the door. The guy came at me, swinging with both fists, his eyes bright with rage.

I set myself.

I nudged a long, looping right out of the way, let him get in close and lifted my fist. It caught him solidly on the chin. His teeth clacked. I brought my left down against his temple. His eyes rolled and he sat down so hard the trailer swayed. He sat there for a moment, head lolling, then sprawled out on his side.

Outside, the hound yelped, circling the trailer in wet gallops. At the sink, I filled the dishpan with water and poured it over the guy's head. He swallowed, grunted, and lay there. I pitched the dishpan into the sink, found a cigarette, lit it, and waited. My hands shook and I was still mad.

"You point a gun at somebody," I said. "You should figure to use it. That's what it's for. Don't just stand there and prove you're a fool."

He grumbled something in a strange language nobody ever heard.

My knuckles were all right. My wrist was sore, but it would go away. The blow had caught him neatly, and I had been lucky.

Three times in my life I'd been up against a similar situation. Guys with guns. Only they used them. One slug was still in my left side. They didn't want to dig for it. It hurt sometimes. The doc said it would eventually work itself out. The guy that did that had died on his feet a moment after shooting me. I didn't like thinking about that.

I leaned over and grabbed the front of his slicker, dragged him to his feet. He was sick-eyed. I shoved him around the table onto the bench.

"What are you to Ivor Hendrix?" I said.

The hound rampaged outside. The guy stared at me.

I reached out and slammed my fist against the side of his face. He tipped over. I sat him up again.

"What are you to Ivor Hendrix?" I said.

His eyes steadied. "A friend."

"What were you doing, sneaking around here?"

"Kind of neighbor," he said. "I was rabbit hunting. I saw your car and thought I ought to investigate."

"You a watchdog?"

His eyes swam, then saw me again.

"What's your name?" I said.

"Gamba. Vince Gamba. I don't know why I'm telling you all this."

"Sure you do."

Behind his eyes he wanted me to believe he was suddenly tired of all this.

He said, "She hasn't been around. I haven't seen her husband lately, either. I *was* kind of keeping an eye on the place."

"You and your dog. You got him trained to kill?"

"Sometimes Buck gets excited."

We watched each other for a moment, like a couple of Jap wrestlers getting set to kick low.

He said abruptly, "Why are you asking me all these things? Who are you? You a cop?"

I said, "You and Carl Hendrix friends?"

"I told you. We're neighbors."

I leaned down and put my face closer to his. "How do neighbors fit in?" I said.

"Damned if I'll tell you anything else."

"You're damned, then." I reached out and took a handful of his soaked hair and wrenched his head back, then rolled the knuckles of my right fist roughly against his jaw. I didn't have the stomach to hit him again.

"He was giving her a raw deal," he gasped. "She's always trying to do right by him. Come on, let go."

I let go. He waved an arm around, indicating the trailer, then said, "Look how he takes care of her."

"Concerned about that, eh?"

He clamped his lips tightly together.

"You answer the telephone, too?" I said.

"I don't get you."

I let that ride. I wasn't sure about his voice, whether he'd been the one who answered the phone here when I called.

"How's he giving her a raw deal?"

Something came over his face. He spoke softly. "Do what you like, I'm not saying anything else till I know who the hell you are."

I took out a card and held it in front of his eyes. He read it, reached for it. I put it away. It jarred him slightly.

"What's happened to her?"

I said, "How's he giving her a raw deal?"

"With that pig."

"What pig?"

"His sister-in-law. Ivor doesn't even know — wouldn't believe it, anyway."

I lit a cigarette and stared at him. The cigarette tasted rotten. I went over by the sink, turned on the faucet and let it extinguish the ember. I popped the garbage can lid with my toe, and dropped the butt inside. There was nothing in the can but a half dozen or so paper airplanes. Some were crumpled as if they'd been hurriedly picked up.

"What's happened?" he said. "Can't you tell me what's happened? Something must've happened."

"Where does Hendrix hang out?" I said.

"Mostly down on First Street, in town. He bums around with a guy named Lager — Joe Lager. They're drinking buddies."

"Who else does he know?"

"I don't know."

"His sister-in-law married?"

He nodded. "A lush. A nympho and a lush."

Outside the dog whined mournfully.

"Get up and get out of here," I said.

He looked at me, puzzled. I took his shotgun out of the sink, turned and tossed it at him. He was half up. He caught it, sat down, then came to his feet.

"Okay," I said. "Out you go."

He walked past me and out of the door. I went over and picked up my slicker, shook it, got it on, flipped the wall switch. I stepped outside, closed and locked the door. He stood there watching me in the fine rain. I pocketed the key.

The hound's ears lifted and he sniffed at the air. His coat was plastered with mud and he was nervous. Abruptly, he turned and galloped for the cement block house.

In the gray light of early darkness, the dog leaped scratching at the closed door of the cement house.

"Come on, Buck — Buck!" Gamba called hoarsely.

The hound turned and looked at him, and for some reason my heart pulled into my throat. The hound had been taught to obey. Finally, it whined along the ground toward its master, keening with clenched teeth.

Vince Gamba turned and walked off toward the lake. He moved over a low knoll. The hound bellied after him. They vanished into the woods.

I could hear him talking to the hound in a low voice, then the world was a wet silence again.

I wondered if he knew about the body. I wondered if he could be the "person" Ivor had refused to name. I wondered what she would do when I told her Carl was dead. I wondered what Haddock was thinking. I wondered what Asa Crafford would tell me.

Did the four hundred thousand tie in? Would it be smart for me to try and crack this thing on my own? Were the gods laughing?

I went back inside the trailer and phoned Hoagy Stills, an old friend, a ballistics expert with the lab crew of the department. He might know some inside dope on the Laketown job. He might tell me. He was at his home, but sleeping. He worked nights and his wife wouldn't wake him. I thanked her through my teeth.

Maybe it would be a good idea to drop the whole thing, go back to the office, and continue with cleaning up the mess my old man had left me. Maybe I should wait for something respectable to walk in my door.

I looked back across the years, searching for something respectable that had occurred to me in this business.

That way lay madness.

FIVE

She sat on the couch and looked stunned.

"Dead," she said softly.

"Somebody had to tell you," I said. "I didn't want you to read it in the papers. As it is, the police will probably locate you before long. I'm sorry."

She kept on staring at me. Her eyes were glazed, and she was pale. She wasn't seeing me. She was looking at something inside her head. The thick auburn hair shone in dull lamplight. She wore a soft aqua robe, belted tightly at the waist with a broad white sash, and except for the stunned expression she was lovelier than ever.

She swallowed slowly. "How could he die?"

This was never easy. "He was murdered."

"I don't understand."

"Somebody didn't want him to go on living, Ivor."

She stood up. The robe opened the full length of long white thigh. She closed it with an absent brush of palm. I had been seated on the chair in front of the couch. I got up and went over to her.

"It's all right," I said foolishly. "Easy, now."

The robe was made of thin soft material that looked wet in places where it clung to her body. There was nothing underneath the robe.

"No," she said. She looked at me with the tragic eyes. The mouth was red and damp and soft, the lips parted. "Don't you see? They'll think I killed him."

I thought of him lying out there and what had been done to him. I had seen plenty dead bodies, enough to pin down how long they'd been dead quite closely, as closely as anybody. "Don't worry about that," I told her as kindly as I could. "You were in Orlando, at Carl's aunt's. He's been dead well over a week. You don't have to worry."

She stepped back. "Over a week? It couldn't be."

"Is, though." I didn't want to detail it. "I'm positive it's not less than eight days."

She was suddenly eager. "It's not Carl."

I reached for her. "Steady."

"I tell you, it's not my husband. I spoke with him on the phone day before yesterday. It was a short conversation — but I *did* talk with him."

I was holding her shoulders. I let go. Neither of us breathed for a moment.

I said, "You told me he wouldn't answer the phone."

"Not since then — day before yesterday. He was very angry — I told you how he acted."

"You're absolutely certain it was your husband?"

"Positive."

She lifted one hand suddenly and touched her face.

"It's Vince," she said softly. "He's killed Vince." She paled. "I'm scared. He's killed Vince, and now he'll kill me." She looked at me. "You've got to stop him. It's plain now — he's trying to find me."

"You mean Vince Gamba?"

She fixed me with quizzical eyes.

"It's not Vince Gamba," I said. "I talked with him, out there. He was — around."

She sat on the couch again. I tried to put myself in her place. It was a bad place to be in. The world had gone cockeyed for her. Nothing added up. I sat beside her.

She said, "Where did you find the dead man?"

I told her.

"What made you think it was Carl?"

I explained about the note I'd found written by her, and told her Carl's wallet was in a pants pocket. She broke in.

"There's something I haven't told you. It didn't mean anything till now. A few days before I left, a man came to see Carl. I don't know who he was, except Carl said he was an old friend. Said his name was Bill Black, but I doubted it then."

"Why?"

"The way he said it, I think. I know Carl didn't like seeing him, at first. The man was sick. He asked Carl to put him up for a while."

"What makes you think Carl didn't want to see him?"

"They argued a lot. Always out of my hearing. Carl wouldn't tell me what about. He can be very close-mouthed. Next thing, they were friends. Carl fixed him a place to stay in the little house you mentioned.

It was fine for a day or so, then they began arguing again. It got pretty bad."

"Why didn't you do something?"

"I asked Carl to tell the man to leave, but he said to forget it. It was real wild, the way they swore at each other."

"This guy Black have any luggage?"

"Two suitcases, yes. He came in his own car."

"Can you describe him?"

"Well — medium. Light hair, shortish. Most of the time he wore a gray suit without a tie. He looked tired and not well. He drove a Ford, kind of beat-up. A light gray two-door sedan, not a late model."

I'd been thinking of the maroon Olds. "What year?"

"Maybe a forty-nine. I'm not good at those things, but I know a forty-nine because I used to drive one."

"Anything distinctive about the car? Maybe a dented fender, something like that?"

She shook her head, then hesitated. "The right front hubcap was missing." She took a deep breath. The front of her robe moved abundantly outward, the open flare of throat separating to reveal the lush tops of large, smooth breasts.

I mentioned the note, wondering if the body could be this Bill Black and how the note and Carl's wallet got into his pocket. "You asked Carl to hit Elk for some dough."

"He owes it to us. Elk and Carl were starting a contracting business. Carl sank everything we had into it." She shrugged. "Elk backed down at the last minute. The money was all gone. He'd spent it. Carl was plenty hot about that."

"He never got any of it."

"Elk put him off. He's had practice."

I checked my watch. "I'm going to have to beat it. Time will count, if I'm going to help you."

"Don't worry about money," she said. "I sold the car after you left this afternoon. I want you to help me — I know you don't work for nothing."

I made no comment. I wanted to ask her a lot of things. There was no time now.

"To think I wanted to go back to him," she said. "I know why. It's because I was afraid. I thought if I could talk to him everything would be all right again."

"Yeah. But he threatened you."

Her fingers clenched on the robe. "It was crazy. I know that now." Her gaze was tight. "You've got to find him before he finds me. I know he means what he said, now."

"You may be right, you may be wrong."

"I don't love him. I never want to see him." She held my gaze. "I'm frightened — it won't go away."

I stood up. "Listen, I want you to go to another hotel, invent a different name, and sign in. Then keep phoning my office, and my home, till you reach me." I gave her my apartment number. "There's a lot more to this than I can explain right now."

She stood up and came close to me.

I asked her about pictures of Carl. She got her purse and took out a jeweled wallet and handed me three snapshots. I put them in my pocket.

"I'm still frightened, Lee," she said. "But you've made me feel an awful lot better. Better than I've felt in years."

I couldn't see why. I'd done nothing. But it was very hard to think of her as a client. I took her hand in both of mine.

"You do as I say," I told her. "As fast as you can. We're a long way into the woods, and we're going deeper. We want to be sure of a way out. Okay?"

"Okay, Lee."

We looked at each other. It was enough to make you lock the doors and pull down the shades. I got the faintest whiff of that perfume again. I let go of her hand, snagged my slicker off the chair, and got out of there fast.

SIX

I turned on the light. The office waiting room hadn't cleaned itself. I closed the door, checking for mail. Six days in the home town had brought nothing to this waiting room except unpaid bills, morning and evening papers, and stray notes of condolence. There was the same creaky rattan furniture I remembered as a kid, and thick dust. I was glad she hadn't come here.

The inner office was worse. I turned on the desk light. I'd been sorting, filing, every day since pulling in from California. Stuffed manila folders were stacked on file cabinets, desk, chairs, everywhere. Loose papers and books littered the floor, along with old tobacco tins, gnawed and broken pipes, a couple of raddled fly swatters, and other aged and even nostalgic junk, like a sack of marbles — selected cat's eyes and steelies I remembered having back in grammar school. My old man had left me a mess.

I sat behind the desk in the old swivel chair. The phone directory was on the floor. I heaved it up on the desk and lit a cigarette.

James Baron was still in this room. A human being doesn't leave a place in which he's lived and worked for over a quarter of a century just because he dies.

For years he'd been after me to throw in with him, help him make something of the agency. I'd been too much of a fool to know for certain that all I wanted to be was a good private cop. So when I finally made up my mind and figured to burst in on him and surprise the hell out of him, he was already three days dead.

I phoned Hoagy Stills' home again. His wife said he was still sleeping. She would appreciate it if I'd cease calling. The ringing phone might wake him.

I checked the directory. There was an Elk Crafford listed at 7 Canawlside Drive, over on Grove Point. I wanted to see him, or his wife. I thought about his wife, remembering her as Ivor's long-legged kid sister. She'd been a pretty wild kid, and I wondered how she'd be now. Thinking about her letters to Carl reminded me I needed a shower.

At my apartment in Bahama Shores, I shaved, took a fast shower, and finally quit thinking about what I'd heard of Asa Crafford. I got dressed. I wore my brown sharkskin and a pair of crepe-soled shoes. I felt wide awake; crisp, hard, hot and hungry.

In the living room, I stared at the phone. It didn't ring. I decided to give it half a chance.

I went through the evening paper. Nothing new on the Laketown robbery. Out in the kitchen, I poured half a water glass full of bourbon, took a swallow, had a flash.

I remembered seeing a large carton of newspapers in a closet down the hall by the fire exit. I got that, hauled it back to the kitchen, and set it on the table.

There was a summing-up story on the Laketown job in a week-old *Journal*. I took my glass of whisky and the paper into the other room, sat in the one comfortable chair facing the big window overlooking Tampa Bay, and started checking.

Close to four hundred thousand dollars. A lolloping sack of jack. Sheriff's Department theorized getaway car headed south, maybe Miami. Whoever pulled it had sure scraped the paint. His one bad slip was creaming a guy named McCarthy, a teller, with a .32. It was hard to figure anybody planning to rob a bank with a .32. Two men in the robbery, so far as was known. They had come up with a fresh witness, a Mrs. Cargy Johnson. Mrs. Johnson said: "I was scared to tell what I saw, but I've been thinking it over. It's really not so much, but I thought it might help. I was in Union Trust Wednesday noon when it was held up and robbed. There were two men. The vault was open, just like the paper said. But what I saw was, they had a big suitcase and that's what they put the money in. A big brown leather suitcase, with leather straps and brass buckles. On the top were small black initials. Just as plain. It looked as if somebody had tried to scrape them off with a knife. They were 'K. S. L.,'" she told the deputies.

My hands were cold as I reread those words. And I was out by that trailer in the rain, kicking tin cans, not a care in the world, staring into the trash pit where they burned things at the large brown leather suitcase, three-quarters burned, with the initials "K.S.—." There had been no "L." That was burned off.

I knew now that I was working for a bigger client than Ivor Hendrix. *I was my own client*. I would help her. But I would help myself, this time. This was big. My chance to set up business.

The phone didn't ring. She would call later.

I shook out my slicker and left. I had coffee and an anemic ham sandwich at a drugstore, then headed for 7 Canawlside Drive.

The streets were slick. The rain had nearly ceased.

To all intents and purposes, as Grandma used to say, Carl Hendrix was dead. In the eyes of the police, until proven otherwise. I decided to play it that way, watch reactions, see what happened, until I learned something. This was mine, straight to the dregs.

I made two fast corners, and that was when I spotted the possible tail. I was about a mile from Seminole Causeway, short-cutting through narrow residential streets, or I might have missed him.

I slowed. He swept in a half block, then cut his speed. All I could see were headlights. I tried to make out the grillwork, but it was no dice. I took it easy for about eight blocks. He stuck. I took a right, then a left, and another right, fast, then eased down again. He showed.

Shoving the gas to the floor, I let it go flat out for three blocks, took a wheel-screaming left, braked, made a U-turn, and parked on the other side of the street. I waited over five minutes. Nothing.

Finally I drove on toward the causeway. You can be mistaken. I'd had it look like a tail before, only to find it was some guy coming home from work.

He came up beside me doing about seventy, with his lights off, on the causeway. I nearly missed spotting him. I braked just as he cut in on me. He nearly went through the rail, and so did I. My engine quit. By the time I got it started, he was gone.

I parked at the curb down a way from the hedge- and tree-shielded house on Canawlside Drive. The neighborhood was a haven of expensive silence. Obviously the payments were kept up. The "canawl" was down the street to the right, guarded by a line of snotty-looking silver oaks, grass-banked and serene.

The rain had ceased. The night was dark, fragrant, cool. I walked past waxen-leafed ligustrum hedging along waferlike imported flags. A meandering drive to the left led between dollar-aged slump-block walls toward a gleaming midnight-colored platform at the entrance.

The air shivered against the distant sound of a woman's laughter, the exclusive clink of ice in a glass.

I punched the bell. Chimes tinkled delicately.

SEVEN

A young woman came down a vast hallway toward the door.

She was tall and every inch, from any distance, an eye-peeler. Thick black hair, lush hips that curved in to one of the narrowest of waists. The black hair was yanked to the left side of her head, shaped to a fold over her shoulder; she looked something like a brunette, well fed, polished, modern Veronica Lake. Her head tilted slightly to the left as if the hair were a bit too heavy to tote. She wore a pale green wrap-around evening get-up, with silver threads running through the cloth. The dress opened in a long narrow V to the black sash around her waist. She wore black, flat-soled slippers that made no sound as she neared across pale marble floor. She carried herself like a hot dream.

The first door opened.

She straddled her late twenties, and if you looked hard, you saw in the shape of her face that she was Ivor's sister.

She opened the door in front of me and flipped a cigarette past my ear. It sparkled high out across the lawn.

"I've decided you can go to hell," she said lightly.

"Will you come with me?"

She stared at me, frowned as if I were a bug caught on the outside of a window screen, then said abruptly, "Oh. You're not—!" She covered her broad red mouth with one hand and laughed gently behind the hand. Her breasts did things under the thin cloth. She took the hand down and said carefully, "I'm sorry. I thought you were my husband."

"Forget it."

We smiled. Her lower lip was sulky. She had changed considerably since I'd last seen her, and none of it was to the bad, if you disregarded a certain obvious harshness.

"Well? What is it?"

I grinned at her. "Asa?" I said. "You don't remember me, do you?"

"I should, shouldn't I. I can tell."

I didn't realize I had changed that much. It was a little discouraging. "Lee Baron," I said.

We stood there and went through some of the sudden bright formalities. We shook hands. Where have you been; It's been such a long time, hasn't it; You haven't changed; Neither have you; This certainly is a surprise; You're married now; Yes, it's crazy, isn't it? "Well," she said. "Whatever brings you here?"

Her face was without expression now. She had things on her mind, and I wasn't among them. Her right palm moved once up, once down her right thigh.

I said, "It's about Carl Hendrix, Asa."

"Oh. What about him?"

"He's dead."

The right corner of her mouth jerked once. That was all. It was enough.

"Come in," she said. She turned and walked into the house, through the doors. She waited for me in the hall, then said, "Follow me."

Her walk was lusciously lazy from behind, mindful of Abbe Lane crossing the platform for a bit of cha-cha-cha.

We left the hall without my knowing it and entered a muted, lushly furnished large room, softly lighted, sprinkled with low couches and chairs. Whoever manufactured the carpet had been thinking of sleeping, not walking.

"Please sit down."

I sat on the edge of an enormous chair. She parked herself on an immense, circular blood-red hassock and leaned on one arm. The fold of hair had slipped inside the V of her dress. She lifted it out and slung it over her shoulder.

"Now," she said quietly. "What's all this?"

I told her again, briefly. "Carl Hendrix is dead."

The corner of her mouth jerked again.

She said, "Why do you come to me?"

"Thought you might be able to help me."

"I still don't get it."

"He was murdered."

There was a large, well stocked, gleaming bar at the far end of the room. She got up and walked over there.

"Care for a drink?" she said.

"No."

She stopped, turned, and looked at me. Then she went to the bar. "I'll have two, then," she said. "I'll make believe you drank the other."

She took a bottle and shot glass, poured the glass full, knocked it down. She did this twice more. Then she returned to the hassock and sat down again.

I said nothing.

"Still asking the same question," she said. "Why come to me?"

"I think you know."

She crossed her legs, pulled her dress open so it hung down either side of her legs, above her knees. She scratched her thigh up near the rim of her sheer stocking, watching me. Fingernails rasped quietly, then ceased. There was a disdainful expression in her eyes. She left her dress that way, watching me. It was all done in a practiced way, almost absently — not quite.

"Now that you've proved to me that you have nice legs, shall we talk?"

"Thanks for the compliment."

"It's my pleasure."

"I like to give pleasure."

"Doesn't it trouble you that you can't give any more to Carl Hendrix?"

She straightened. "Just exactly what do you mean by that?" Her eyes widened. Her dress began to slide open still more. She stood up quickly, leaned toward me from the waist. "I think you'd damned well better explain yourself, and fast," she snapped. "And then I think you'd better get the hell out of here even faster."

I sat there. I watched her.

I felt nasty. She had done it. They dangle it in front of you, then when you reach for it, they yell. I wondered if she would yell.

"I read the letters," I said. "He never burned them."

She held the pose.

"Does that trouble you?" I said. "Does it make you any more human?"

"One of those," she said, straightening. "Another one of those goddamned creeps."

"There were three letters. I read every line."

You could see things happening behind her eyes.

"Hottest stuff I ever read," I said. "Wowers."

She came at me with her claws. I got up fast and met her halfway. She kicked for my shins. The claws were like an eagle's. Down in her throat, she was screeching. I'd triggered a bomb.

I snapped out and grabbed her wrists. She was strong and mad. She kept trying to kick me. I twisted her arms behind her, got in tight against her so she couldn't kick, and looked into her eyes. She'd been crocked all the time, I saw it now. I held her that way, talked into an explosive aroma of rare old brandy.

"Hold still and shut up," I said. "I came here with the idea I could talk to you. I wasn't going to mention those letters."

"Oh, no — of course not!"

She socked me with her hips. Her thighs writhed. She stomped on my feet, and the throat of her dress pulled back across a plump bare breast. I held her wrists in the small of her back and squashed her flat against me so she couldn't move. Her body was a curved hunk of hell.

She went limp. She looked at me, her face an inch from mine, her eyes foggy.

A man spoke from the hallway entrance. I turned my head, but I didn't let go of her.

He said, "Don't mean to interrupt. Only bother you a minute. Excuse me."

He crossed the room, not looking at us. A large man wearing a white dinner jacket and black tie. He carried a pipe. He walked stiffly to the bar, picked up a bottle, turned and walked back toward the hall. He didn't speak again. I listened to him walking down the hall, and a door closed.

"Who was that?"

"My husband."

"Shall I let you go now?"

"Try it."

I tried another tack. "This isn't going to get either of us anywhere. All I want to do is ask you a couple of questions. I won't mention the letters again."

I let go of her and gave her a push. She sat down hard on the hassock. She sat there staring up at me for a moment. She fixed her dress. She breathed heavily.

I didn't say anything.

She put her elbows on her knees, put her head in her hands, looking down at her lap. "I'm sorry," she said. "I'm all mixed up. It doesn't really matter, because everything's a mess anyway."

I tried breathing regularly. It worked.

She held her head that way, not looking up. "What do you want to ask me?" she said. "Go ahead. I don't give a goddam."

"When did you last see Carl Hendrix?"

"A week or so ago."

"Where?"

"In my bedroom."

"What about your husband? Doesn't he count?"

"He counts."

"That's not an answer."

"Sorry, again. I'm always sorry. I spend my life being sorry. That's how I get my kicks. Being sorry."

"That still doesn't answer my question."

"You're a real tough onion, aren't you?"

"If you say so. Why don't you stop knocking yourself and talk with me? You're not the only one who has it rough."

"No?"

"No."

"I'd like to see somebody match me."

"So would I."

She lowered her hands and looked up at me. "Okay, Lee. You win. Funny. They always win."

"Yeah. Very funny. Ever since the first time under the front porch."

"How did you ever guess?"

"I didn't guess. I was there, don't you remember?"

"You weren't the guy who started me off."

I grinned sadly at her. "Maybe not, but maybe I was the one who made it fun."

She shot me a timid, half-embarrassed smile. Then her face changed. She put her head in her hands again. "So why did you go away? Why did you leave me there? I'm still under that goddamned porch."

I went over and sat down in the chair. She looked across at me, the black hair hanging down one side of her face, her head propped on one hand now.

I said, "Why did you get so excited over those letters?"

"Where are they?"

"I tried to tell you before. This isn't going to get us anywhere. You'll have to answer my questions, or it won't work."

She looked away. "Sorry." She sat there like that, a very beautiful woman, and mixed up. "I guess I don't want to discuss those letters any more."

"You saw Carl a week or so ago, in your bedroom."

"Yes."

"Does your sister know about you and Carl?"

"Ivor? Dear, sweet Ivor? No, I don't believe she knows."

"Do you think she might have found out?"

She looked at me again and licked her lips.

I said, "You think if she found out, she might want to do something about it?"

"Like killing Carl?"

I shrugged.

She dropped her hand, put both hands together, and spaded them between her thighs. She thrust the dress between her thighs. "I suppose it could happen."

"Nothing much excites you."

"Some things do. Things that are directly concerned with me." She slid around on the hassock until she was facing me in the chair again. She leaned back on her elbows. "I'm very selfish. All I care about are sensations."

"You have a lot of them."

"No. I'll never have enough."

"What are we getting at?"

"I want to sleep with you."

The room warmed. It was as if somebody had turned on the furnace.

I said, "Sex is everything."

"To me, it is. For instance, I want you, and I'm going to get you."

"What about him?" I nodded toward the hall.

"Elk? He's all right. He's fine. Don't worry about Elk. There's no shim-shamming. He knows what I like. When I married him, I told him I'd never be happy sleeping just with him."

"Yet, he married you anyway?"

She nodded. "Yes, you see Elk's a kind of a poet. He's still very much in love with Carol. I look an awful lot like Carol. Practically the spitting image. I'll show you a picture sometimes."

"Who's Carol?"

"His first wife."

"Where does the poetry come in?"

"She's been dead for seven years."

I said nothing for a moment.

She said, "Shall we go up to my room, now?"

"Not now."

"I can wait. If you don't make me wait too long. Then I get nasty." She hesitated. "Actually," she said. "I'm very surprised and sorry to hear about Carl. I mean, someplace, I do feel sorry about it. It just doesn't make me jump up and down with horror, for some reason. My selfishness again, I suppose — I was tired of him." She shrugged. "I don't suppose that's normal."

I still said nothing.

She said, "Who found him?"

"I did."

"Where?"

I told her about it, in detail. She didn't blink.

"That's pretty awful," she said. "I'd rather not hear any more about it. I'm beginning to react to it."

I stared at her.

"I don't want to dream about it," she said. "I can think of much pleasanter things."

"Asa, could I use your phone?"

"You can use anything I've got, darling."

"You're plastered. The phone will do. For now."

"I'm going to be plastereder. In the hall."

I got up and went into the hall. The telephone was in a small alcove. I called Hoagy Stills' home. His wife came on hard and fast and bright with the information that the last time I'd called, the phone ringing woke him. She began taking me apart. I heard a bottle neck clink against a glass from the Crafford living room. A man's voice reached me over the phone. Small argument. Gasp.

"Hello?"

"This is Lee Baron, Hoagy. Sorry to bust up the household like this."

More asides. Two more gasps. Hoagy and I had gone to school together. He was a smart gee. We'd had lunch together three days ago, talking over old times. If I couldn't get anything from him now I might have to start consulting the crystal ball.

"All right, Lee. What is it?"

"You can go back to sleep in a sec," I said. "Tell Jane I'll buy her a box of candy."

"She's on a diet. What is it?"

I asked him if he had any inside stuff on the Laketown robbery; names and faces in particular.

"Whyn't you go see Garlik?"

"Wouldn't be judicious, at present. But it would be extremely judicious on your part if you keep this phone call all to yourself. Now, any old raveled shred will help."

Silence.

"Hoagy?"

"Yeah. You make my nose itch. It's a bad sign."

"Oh, for Christ's sake, come down off the roof."

"I'm with the lab. Whyn't you talk with one of the busy little boys in blue?" he hedged.

"Whyn't you cut this crap? You know something."

"There was an APB this morning to watch for a guy named Barton Yonkers. Broke out of Raiford a while back. Somebody in Laketown came up with a description that seemed to tally. I think it's malarky. Some pigeon at Raiford told the warden Yonkers was planning to meet a guy outside on some deal. That's about it."

"What's this Yonkers' description?" I asked.

"I don't know."

"Who was he meeting?"

"Don't know that, either."

I sighed and scratched my chin. "Okay, Hoagy."

"Oh, there was one other thing. Not much, though."

"What's that?"

"The bulletin said this guy Yonkers was a sick man."

I stopped scratching my chin, told him again that I'd buy him a bottle of rum if he'd keep quiet about talking with me, hung up, and returned to the Crafford receiving room.

"Hi!"

She was on the hassock, very bright-eyed. I sat in the chair and looked at her.

I said, "Your sister told me Carl had a visitor recently. Said they didn't get along. Name of Bill Black."

"Oh?"

"Meet him?"

She frowned faintly, moved her head slowly from side to side. "Nope. Never heard of him, never saw him." She paused, still frowning. "Strange Carl never mentioned him." She smiled. "Probably Ivor had a dream."

"Maybe. Then again, there's the possibility Carl's

not even dead."

Red lips parted across very white teeth. "I'm beginning to think you just wormed your way in here with a tall story."

"Yeah. Ever hear of anybody named Yonkers?"

"Yonkers. No, I don't know anyone by that name. Why?"

"Nothing. Why don't you and your sister get along?"

"Simple. Did we ever? I'm sure you remember. She always had everything. I never had anything. She had you, didn't she?"

"Come off it."

"Well, I still resent her. She always got the boy friends. So I took them away from her." She paused. "I took them under the porch, where she wouldn't go. It was fun, but it didn't do any good."

"Can you think of any enemies Carl might have?"

"I think we really should go up to my room."

"Maybe I agree. But not right now."

She said, "What man worth his salt hasn't enemies?"

"Have you seen your sister lately?"

She smiled broadly. She crossed her legs and opened the dress over her knees again, letting it hang down the sides of her legs. The slit of the dress went up beyond the taut rims of her stockings. Plump white flesh was dented by the stockings and tight black garters.

Her eyes got sly. "Say. Was it you I spoke to earlier on the phone about Ivor?"

I pressed my fingers into the arms of the chair. "No."

She scowled. "Somebody phoned earlier tonight. A man. He asked for Ivor — he was trying to locate her.

I told him I didn't know where she was and cared less. He said his name was Caramba, something like that. Sure that wasn't you?"

"Was the name Gamba?"

"That's it. It was you."

"No. He say anything else?"

"Said to tell Ivor to meet him at the Royal Palms Apartments. Said to tell her if I saw her. I asked him where that was. He said she'd know, that he'd be waiting. He said it was very important, or he wouldn't have bothered me." She paused, fussing with the top of her stocking.

I stood up, looking at her legs. "Aside from your affair with Carl, did Elk have any reason to hate him?"

"They didn't get along, I'm afraid. Elk's hardly dependable. Carl should have known that." She told me briefly what Ivor had said about the two men going together in a contracting business, and how Elk had goofed. "You aren't leaving?"

"Yeah. The cops will probably be here any minute. I don't want to be around."

"Cops?"

"Uh-huh."

"Oh."

She got up and moved over to me.

"I wish to hell you wouldn't go, Baron." I remembered that she sometimes used to call me by my last name. She looked at me steadily. "I mean it."

"I wish to hell I didn't have to go. I mean that, too."

"Will you come back?"

I looked into the shining, frantic eyes. "You're lonely."

"Yes." She smiled. "Kiss me, at least."

I took her in my arms and kissed her. She pressed tightly in against me, moving her lips, a lot of things. Time quivered. I released her forcibly, holding her by the slim waist, feeling the way she stirred. We looked at each other through the smoke. They were quite a pair of sisters.

"Lonely," I said.

"It's what you are of the moment," she said. "The moment's all that counts."

"You need a spanking."

"That's not all."

I turned fast.

"Lee?"

I looked at her.

"There's more to it, Lee. It's Elk — he keeps me cooped up here — I can't — "

"Can't what?"

"Nothing. Go away. But come back."

I looked at her for another moment. Her face had changed subtly. I turned and walked out along the marble hall. I could hear her breathing back there.

In a short time I'd got to know Asa Crafford pretty well. Or was it not at all? Why is it, the minute you get rolling you find everybody hates everybody else enough to kill?

I let myself out quickly. He was sitting on the outside steps, his feet in the drive. He was smoking his pipe, holding the bottle on his knee. He was middle-aged, and his hair was thinning. I wanted to talk with him badly. He glanced up at me, then down at his pipe.

"Nice night," he said gruffly. He had a growling voice.

"It is a nice night," I agreed. I couldn't say anything

else.

"Never mind," he said, thumbing the coal in his pipe. "Never mind."

I walked on out across the drive and started along the flags toward my car. Turning, I looked back at those glass doors. Elk Crafford was walking inside. I saw her standing in the hall where I had left her.

Crafford slammed the outside door. The glass seemed to balloon. Asa Crafford turned, caught at her skirts, and ran toward a long low stairway at the end of the hall. She ran up the stairs. Elk Crafford walked deliberately down the hall, moving with long swift strides. His shoulders tensed. The faint sound of his shout reached me. He ran up the stairs.

There was no sound. Not even a small wind.

I walked back to the curb and stood beside the car. There was an easy way to read this thing. I couldn't believe it was the right way. Too much dream stuff. You could say Yonkers did know Hendrix. Yonkers was Black. He came alone to the trailer after robbing a bank in Laketown, Florida. He needed a place to lie low. Hendrix found out about the money, or maybe he was even in on it. He might have been the unnamed guy the stoolie said Yonkers planned to meet after he crashed Raiford. So Hendrix killed Yonkers for the money. Then what? What would anybody do? They would take a fast plane for South America, or wherever, and that would be that. It did not sound right.

Because why was somebody trying to get me off this thing? If there was four hundred grand, where was it?

I slid under the wheel of the car, and sat there a moment, with the door open. I lit a cigarette. The tobacco smoke was good. I ate it like a fiend. Finally, I reached out to close the door and a man spoke quietly.

"Let's talk."

EIGHT

He had been standing somewhere to the rear of the car, then stepped up as I got in. He was by the open door.

"Go away," I said. "I don't want to talk."

He breathed patiently.

"Slide over, cowboy," he said.

I turned my head and bumped my nose against cold steel, smelling of powder solvent; Hoppe's No. 9 Nitro. "No Marksman Or Hunter Should Ever Be Without It."

I took a better look at him. It wouldn't have done any good to start the car, throw it into gear, and try a run for it. He could have detained a Mack truck with one pinky while balancing a cup of tea on his knee and never spilled a drop. He hulked down, staring at me, with the gun in his fist.

He wore a light, floppy coat, a soft hat, and he had a face the size of a watermelon. Large blunt features, the nose broad and shaped like a loaf of bread, the jaws jutting and wide.

I slid across the seat. He jammed himself in, twined one enormous tentacle around the steering wheel, rested the other on the seat back. The gun was on the end of the seat back. A .45. The polished muzzle gleamed. It was a toy in his hand.

I remembered the face.

"You drive a maroon Olds," I told him.

He didn't say anything. I couldn't see his face now, but he was watching me. He breathed like a wounded bear.

"Goons are passé," I said.

He made a sound like laughter.

He spoke in a mild, intelligent, well educated voice.

"I'm not supposed to be sitting here, like this," he said. He sighed. It was like a horse blowing after a hard run. There's something about really big guys. I mean really big. I'm six-three, and on the lean side but still no shrimp by normal standards. But the big guys, like this one. It's as if they're so clogged up with meat and muscle they can't breathe. They're always gasping and grunting and heaving around. He said, "I'm supposed to either wreck you or just beat you up." He sighed again. "I wanted to see what I'm doing all this to."

"You're the dark ghost that tried to run me off the bridge."

"Yes. The way you pulled out of that made me curious. I suppose that's my one weakness on my jobs. Curiosity toward my marks."

He was imported stock. An expensive heavy. There was no fear in him. Someplace he probably had a wife and children who thought he was maybe a rug salesman. A nice home, with large rooms.

If I got the door open and ran, he would shoot me in the back of the head.

"How much do they pay you?" I said. My throat was dry, my voice hoarse.

"They pay well," he said. "That reminds me." He unwound his left arm, reached inside his coat, and tossed an envelope on my lap.

I looked at the envelope. Three crisp C-notes. I tossed my cigarette out the window, tossed the envelope back in his lap. I didn't have a gun with me.

"Better keep it," he said. "It's kind of a payoff, I suppose. I don't exactly understand it myself. Maybe you're supposed to use it for bills."

"What bills?"

"The ones you'll have to pay after I finish with you."

"Cut it out. This is comic."

"I know," he said. "That's the way I look at it. Then again, it's a bit sad, too. I don't enjoy it. I have a degree in medicine." He sighed. "I'd give anything to be practicing. I worked hard for that. I don't like this at all. It pays well, though, and it's a last straw."

"What the hell are you trying to give me?"

"Truth. Maybe the rain depressed me."

"Why don't you practice, then?"

He made the sound of laughter. "I tried. For nearly five years. Almost starved to death. Hardly worthwhile." He reached over and turned on the dash map light. "Take a look," he said. "Look at this face."

I took a close look. It was pretty bad. A bit like one of the gargoyles on Notre Dame cathedral. He was the ugliest guy I'd ever seen. I looked away. He turned off the map light.

"Patients were just like that," he said. "They never said anything. Didn't want to hurt my feelings. But they couldn't stand it, either. That way with everything I ever tried — I tried everything. I'm right for this job. It's my work."

"Plastic surgery," I said.

He sighed again. "No good. It's the size. It begins with a glandular condition in early childhood. Nothing you can do about it."

I began to breathe with only the upper third of my lungs.

"I know you're scared," he said. "You should be. There's nothing you can do."

"Take the money back," I said. "Give it to whoever sent you and tell them to buy breakfast with it."

"I told them it wasn't enough."

"Did you cut his arms off?"

He didn't speak.

"Where's Carl Hendrix?" I said. "Did you bury him, or what?"

He said nothing.

"Bill Black," I said hoarsely.

He cleared his throat. "I wouldn't continue, if I were you," he said. "I'm not supposed to kill you this round. But I might have to."

I made my voice hard and tight. It was a damned difficult thing to do. "Who comes into the loot? Go ahead, you can tell me."

"You're a stranger in these parts, Baron. You don't know what's been going on. You don't know how to play the game."

I had my hand on the door handle, ready to shove, and make a break. There was nothing else to do.

"Yeah?" I said. I shoved the door handle slowly. "So

what?" I gave a good shove.

He showed me so what. It was thunder. My head exploded with soft white soundless light. My face cracked against the dashboard. Sound and pain came in bright airless waves, then a roaring set in, and above the roaring, his voice — mild, apologetic.

"The idea is," he said, "for you to work on something else. Just put your present job out of your mind. You understand?"

His hand hadn't traveled more than a foot, with the .45 in it, against the back of my head. It struck again. I smashed against the floorboards. I was no longer sane.

I was paralyzed.

I tried to fight back. It was hopeless. I was dreaming. I couldn't move. I was trying to chin myself on the dashboard.

He brought his arm down again. My head fell off.

I yelled at him. I heard myself scream.

I fought with the brake pedal. He was hurting the hell out of me. I knew it was the brake pedal, but felt sure it was the guy, too. I twisted it, then wormed along the floor of the car and ran. I fell on my face in the wet grass. Pain was like scalding water. I tried to get up, succeeded.

I was alone with the night.

By the car, I slid down, hanging to the open door. I sprawled under the car, half off the curb. Everything went away.

I breathed the damp air. There was an odor of damp bricks, damp earth, oil and rubber. I had asked for this. My ears rang and ached. Everything became crazy, with me flying through the middle of it.

Then no sound. I was deaf.

Then I was all right. It was just the night.

He was gone. The Crafford house was dark. The street was dark, except for one light on the far corner, shining like blinding snow under the car where I lay.

I moved slowly. I was a sick old man. The pain was straight down the middle of my back, its roots in my head. I knelt on the grass beside the car. Finally I got on my feet. I fell in across the car seat and lay with my face mashed against crinkling paper. The envelope with the money. I didn't have the strength to pull it free and heave it from the car.

Pain broke away in small chips, like stale icing off a cake. Knives probed me all over while hammers banged on my head.

I waited.

Everything that had happened since I'd found that body a few hours before swamped my mind. Finally I pulled myself up, got hold of the wheel, sat there. I felt my head. It was tender. The skin was broken in places. In other places it felt pulpy, like a bruised apple. Bumps were forming. The guy had been a pro, or he would have killed me.

I started the engine, drove slowly up the street to a short white bridge that arched the canal. I stopped the car, got out, slid down the bank till I stood on sandy soil beside water. The water shone blackly. I knelt and bathed my head and face. The water was refreshing. There wasn't much blood. There was blood on the sleeve of my jacket. I washed it off, and returned to the car.

I'd been right. This case was going to be a toughie. I felt fairly certain that the dead guy was Barton Yonkers. Proof would have to wait. I had to make my play across enough of a ditch from the hometown cops so they couldn't take direct action to stop me. If they did, I was done.

In the glove compartment, I got out the aspirin bottle, swallowed five. The Dexedrine was gone. I remembered using it up days ago, driving across the country, in a hurry to get home.

To this.

NINE

I heard the phone ringing as I came down the hall toward my apartment. I ran, got the key in the lock, opened the door, and dove across the room through the dark, expecting the ringing to cease.

I grabbed the phone off the cradle.

"Mr. Baron?"

It was Ivor Hendrix. "Yeah." I carried the phone over to the chair and sat in the darkness. The night was very black beyond the window, with a freighter crawling through the middle of it; tiny saffron cabin lights, running lights. A dreamship in black space. I knew she was on Tampa Bay, headed for the Gulf of Mexico, but she seemed airborne. I ached all over, and the aspirin hadn't helped my head.

"I thought I'd never talk to you again," she said.

I felt the lumps on my head.

She said, "I imagined all sorts of things. I've been

trying to reach you for so long." Worry edged her voice. "Do you honestly think Carl might be — after me?"

"I don't know," I said. "Where are you?"

"Another motel. I did as you asked. It's called Shady Nook. On Maranela Street, North." She gave me the address and phone number. "I signed as Grace Golden."

"Okay, Miss Golden. You've seen no one who knew you?"

"No."

"Good. I want you to stay there. Don't go out unless you absolutely have to."

"Now you *are* scaring me. Will you please tell me what this is all about? I'm worried, and I'm scared."

"I'm afraid a lot of things happened while you were up in Orlando."

"What sort of things?" Her voice leveled, and she spoke more quietly. "Please," she said. "I have a right to know — is Carl after me, or what? There's something you're not telling me. Don't try to keep things from me. I'm all alone in this horrible little room."

"Okay." She would know soon enough. I had no idea whether the police had found the paper currency band from the Laketown Union Trust. If they hadn't found it, they would assume the body was that of Carl Hendrix, and the entire state would be alerted to pick up his wife. If they *had* discovered the lead, they still would want her. Every moment that went by pushed me a little deeper into the bog. "When you were in Orlando, you probably heard about the bank robbery in Laketown?"

"Sure," she said. "Aunt Liz had money in that bank. She was in an uproar. What's that got to do with this?"

"I don't know yet. It sure as hell enters in somewhere." I told her about the currency band I'd found. "And there's this Bill Black you said visited Carl. I don't think that's his real name any more than you do. And the fact remains, that body still might be your husband."

She was anxious now. "You should be able to tell quickly. I gave you those pictures of Carl."

"Hold on a sec." I put the phone down, turned on a light, and went into the bedroom. I got the snapshots from the jacket pocket of my other suit. I'd forgotten about them. Back in the chair, I picked up the phone, looking at the pictures. They didn't tell much, and they never could because of the way the corpse's face had been hatcheted.

In the photos, Carl Hendrix was a medium tall guy with short hair and an ordinary-looking face, wearing a short-sleeved sports shirt. He stood by a palm tree in one shot, staring soberly at the camera. His eyes seemed to pop slightly, indicating a possible thyroid condition. It might ease identification problems. The other two snaps were of him seated in a lawn chair, smoking a cigarette in a stubby white holder. I couldn't place the surroundings.

"Are you there?" she said hesitantly.

"Yeah. Checking the photos. They don't tell me anything." I explained why.

"How awful." She paused, then said, "But why would — the arms be ... ?"

"Well, figure it this way. Say you have a dead man

on your hands, and you don't want to be caught. You've got to get rid of the body. That's always a problem. Believe me, I've seen some weird attempts. The present job is hardly original. It's the one real reason I don't think the dead man is your husband."

"But why?"

"Too much concern over making the body unidentifiable. If whoever killed him simply buried the body, there's a damned good chance of it being found. It often is — usually somebody sees the killer burying it, or doing whatever he does with it. So whoever it was decided on another tack. They got rid of the arms — it could have been merely the hands. Fingerprints, see?"

"I'm beginning to."

"And they also raised a lot of havoc with the facial characteristics. It'll take time for identification. No telling where the arms are. If the police had the arms, the hands, they could find out damned quick who the guy really is."

"I suppose so. Don't the photos help at all?"

"It could be your husband out there. On the other hand, it could be ten thousand other guys."

"But — if it isn't Carl, then who is it?"

"Maybe this guy Bill Black. Listen, when was the last time you burned stuff in that trash pit behind the trailer?"

"I don't remember. Maybe just before I went away. Carl may have burned things since."

"Specifically. Did this guy Black burn anything?"

"Not that I now of."

"Maybe you can remember. Had the Laketown

robbery occurred before or after you arrived at Carl's aunt's?"

"Before. A day or so, a few days. I remember, because Aunt Liz was hopping about it when I got there."

"Have you ever heard the name Yonkers?"

She paused. "As a person? No."

"What was Carl's work when he was working?"

"Well, he's a CPA. Sometimes he'd work at that. I mean, he was employed for short periods. He hasn't worked at anything steady for nearly two years. Just odd jobs. Carpentry — and loafing."

"What did you live on?"

"He had saved some money. And he played the horses some. He was lucky once in a while. He took odd jobs. We managed to get along. Elk took the savings money."

"Somebody, you or your husband, made paper airplanes. Who was that?" I told her of discovering some in the refuse container by the sink.

"That would be Carl, yes. It was a habit."

"What is Elk's line of work?"

She gave a short, brittle laugh. "He inherited some money. A lot. It's all gone, or nearly. He's never worked seriously at anything, unless it's trying not to work. Now I suppose he'll have to. I'm sure they have next to nothing."

"I just came from talking with your sister."

"Oh. Why?"

"Thought she might help."

"I'm sure she helped." The words were lathered with sarcasm.

"She's not a very happy person."

"She tries awfully hard."

I let it go. It was leading to dark nooks I wasn't concerned with at the moment.

I said, "She told me Vince Gamba was trying to reach you. He's staying at the Royal Palms Apartments. She said he phoned her."

Ivor Hendrix was silent.

"If there's anything you haven't told me about that," I said. "Maybe you should."

"There's nothing. There never was anything. It's all over now. I mean it."

"What does Gamba do?"

"He's some sort of a salesman."

My head was really painful. The room skidded, then righted itself. I felt rotten. I needed a drink.

I said, "You stay where you are. I'll contact you. If you need me for anything, call either the office or here. Keep trying till you get me."

"I wish you'd come and see me."

"I can't right now. I'd like to."

"I'd like you to."

"Soon as I can. All right?"

"All right."

I hung up and headed dizzily for the kitchen and the whisky bottle. I poured a water glass half full, started drinking it, and the telephone rang.

It was Vince Gamba. He was very drunk. He was so cockeyed it was all I could do to understand him. He was trying very hard to be deathly serious, which can be alarming. He sounded close to tears.

"Try get you long time," he said. "Try phone — drunk."

"I gather that," I said.

"'Pol 'gize. 'Pol 'gize being such ass — afternoon."

"Okay."

His voice was tight and desperate through the alcohol. He was so anxious the phone practically shook in my hand. He wanted to say something but couldn't find the right approach.

"Mus' see you."

"Now?"

"No." He began to speak with strenuous slowness. "Give — me — two — hour — z-z-z. Sober up, two hours. You come — my — place. Roy — le — oily — all, ah, Jesus! ROY — LEY — ALL — "

"Royal Palms Apartments?"

"How you know?"

"Me Magwa, much crystal ball."

Silence. "You fun."

"Yeah. Me fun. Heap blast. Ugh."

He sounded as if he were crying; either that or choking to death.

He belched, then slobbered, "Jeeze-*CHRI*sags! The money. Money beared — braided — "

"Buried?" A cold clamp tightened on the back of my head.

"Yes. Know where buried, think. Two hours."

"Wait." I heard my voice, like wire. "Wait, Gamba. Tell me what you know, man, *now.*"

"Must talk you firs'. Two hour."

Damn the fool. "Where are you — home?"

"No. Sober up. Be home."

"Goddamn it, tell me!"

He hung up.

I heard voices mumbling in the hall before the knock.

Then the knock on the door. A demanding knock. I was already halfway out of the chair. I turned off the light, cursed myself for doing it, and drifted like pale smoke to the door.

"The light went out," a man said.

Another man started to say something. I didn't wait to see what it was. I moved fast to the kitchen, let myself out the service door that led into a hall at right angles with the main hall leading to the front door. I skimmed silently down the hall and looked around the corner. Four flatfeet. They were knocking again. I didn't want to talk with those guys for a while.

I went back down the hall, closed the kitchen door with the latch on, then headed for the Fire Exit.

My head was a solid square yard of throbbing pain.

TEN

Driving slowly down Tangerine Avenue, I took the three crisp C-notes from the envelope and put them in my wallet. I wadded up the envelope and tossed it out the window. What point arguing?

If and when I again met watermelonpuss, he would be repaid three hundred dollars' worth of knuckles. It was all a matter of getting the drop. I would get the drop.

Somehow I had to find out for certain who the dead man was. I had to stay ahead of the police. I didn't like the idea of the men in blue being this warm on me. Maybe Haddock had merely sent them around for a chat.

I stopped at a drugstore, gulped a double Bromo for the head. It didn't seem to help. Maybe I was concussed. The thought of buried money could concuss anybody. The counter clerk stared at me. I saw myself in the mirror. He began sorting menu cards, red-necked.

Back in the car, I lit a cigarette, decided it was still too soon to head for Vince Gamba's.

What Gamba had said made me nervous. Then I remembered his telling me about Carl Hendrix's drinking buddy, Joe Lager. They hung out on First Street.

Joe Lager, the beer drinker. A long shot if there ever was one.

I parked the car near first and began checking bars. In the Oriental Tavern, the barman told me Joe Lager was in a back room. The barman seemed irritated. When he spoke Lager's name, he made a face like a hooked mackerel.

I went through a door he pointed out, then down a narrow hall. The hall stank. There was a door at the right, near the end of the hall. I knocked.

"What you want, Meathead?"

"It's not Meathead," I said. "Guess again."

"Oh."

I waited. He opened the door cautiously. I stepped against the door and moved inside before he could slam it. He stepped lightly backward toward an old iron bed, watching me. The room was bare and neat.

"What's up?" he said.

He stared at me. He had smooth brown skin and

silky black hair trimmed so carefully you knew some barber went through hell every week or so. He wore a white sports shirt, dark slacks, brown suede shoes. He had a taut smile that didn't show in his eyes. He probably carried a knife.

I said, "You're a friend of Carl Hendrix's. I'm trying to locate him."

He wasn't sure whether I was the law. It troubled him. Trouble would always be in his eyes, darkly lurking. He sat down on the bed. His eyes were like daubs of ink-soaked cotton.

I said, "You're acting as if you knew something, Joe."

He sat there as if he were carved from a large cake of brown laundry soap.

"This where you live, Joe?"

He showed me one palm. "Who's this Carl Hendrix you're gassing about? So, this is where I live. What right you got, barging in here?"

I started walking around the room. I didn't turn my back enough to count. Only his eyes moved. On the other side of the bed I knew I didn't have to look any more. I leaned down, glanced under the bed. I saw four more of them.

"You like to make paper airplanes, Joe?"

"What the hell you talking about?"

I picked up one of the paper airplanes, creased it good, and came back. I stood in front of him and threw the paper airplane into his face. It bounced off his nose. He didn't move.

"Where is he, Joe?"

He came off the bed, tore into me like a savage. He was trying to get out of the room. I grabbed him around the throat and threw him back on the bed. He lay there a moment, then twisted and ran off the other side of the bed. He came along the foot, then charged for the door. I brought my left fist around. I struck his stomach. He bent around my fist, clawing at my arms. Then he held his stomach, walked backward, and sat down on the bed again.

"Tell me about it," I said.

He got cunning. Gears meshed. He straightened his shoulders and began to nod his head. I stepped back to let him think it over. His hand flashed inside his shirt and he came at me, all in one long crazy movement, the knife poised, glinting in the light from an overhead bulb.

He was fast. He had the knife raised overhead. That should have tipped me. I was a moment late. They don't use them that way. It was a feint. I went for his wrist. The knife wasn't there. It arced to his other hand, and I saw the arm come at me from down under, his face like a paper clown's. The knife shot. I doubled, spinning for the wall. The blade spun past me and socked into the door.

He looked startled. He dove for the knife hilt. I stretched, stepped out, and clubbed him on the back of the head with both fists fingered together. Once, twice, three times, meaning to hurt him.

He fell down and lay on the floor. His eyes were open. I lifted my foot and slowly lowered it over his face.

"Where is he, Joe?"

"I don't know. The dirty bastard owes me. I figured to come here tonight and sweat it out, then when he showed, I'd make him pay up." I thought for a moment he would cry. "He owes me. I fixed this pad for him."

"You're not being too clear, Joe."

He stared up at me. "All I know's his name's Carl Hendrix. What'd he do?"

"I think you're holding."

"What'd he do?"

I tried something for size. "He died."

His eyes changed. They became sick.

"Tell me everything you can, Joe. Maybe I'll be able to ease things a little."

He groaned softly. "He looked me up three weeks ago. Said he had to have a place to stay where nobody'd ask questions. Said could I fix him up. He'd pay me five hundred bucks."

Distant bells chimed. "Say where he got the money?"

"No. Don't think I didn't work on him. Not a peep. He'd been flat, too — so he came by it quick an' easy. I figured he's copped something. I would latch on. I told Eb, the guy who owns this joint, told him I had a friend hiding from his wife, would he arrange? I cut him in and paid the first month's rent. The bastard never showed. Eb said he was here, but I never seen him. Today I figured I'd hang here till he showed. The bastard." He blinked slowly. "Who cooled him?"

"Who said he was cooled?"

"You think I'm stupid?"

I didn't say anything. He didn't, either. Finally, I said, "You ever meet Hendrix's sister-in-law? Asa Crafford?"

His face became consciously blank. "Who?"

"You know who," I said.

"No," he said. "Who?"

"Maybe we could sign on at the Little Theater as a couple of owls," I said. "Or would you rather wear your nose on the back of your head?" I lifted my foot.

"I met her once."

"With Hendrix?"

He nodded. His head thumped the floor.

I said, "I lied to you, Joe. Carl Hendrix isn't dead. You know that, don't you? So we were lying to each other. I wanted to see how you acted. Now I'll know if you're telling the truth. When did you last see Yonkers?"

His brown coloring turned gray.

He said, "You jammed it that time." He spoke softly. Something like strength had come into his eyes. "You're not a cop. I don't give a damn what you do to me. Mash my face in, go ahead. I'm done talking."

"You know I don't believe that, Joe."

"Try. Go ahead. Try."

"I hope you don't think I think you were in Laketown with Yonkers," I said.

He pressed his lips together and showed me how tight together they were.

"Somebody's dead," I said. "You can figure that one out, can't you? A corpse, Joe — without any arms. A very sad trick, don't you think?"

I went over to the door. "Joe?" I said.

His eyes focused on me. I reached over and took hold of his knife sticking into the door panels. I bent the handle down till the blade snapped. It was a strong blade. I tossed the broken hilt on his chest. He didn't move. I said, "If you're thinking of doing anything you consider smart after I leave, don't."

I left the Oriental Tavern.

It was close to nine-thirty. I drove to a drugstore, trying to keep my head from falling off. I was sick to my stomach, and that worried me. I kept thinking about concussion. There was a haze over my eyes.

The pharmacist sold me some large yellow pills with an unpronounceable name, for my head. "Ordinarily," he said, "you need a prescription for these, but I can see you're in trouble."

"It shows."

He told me to take one of the pills. I took four with a glass of water at the counter. By the time I was back in the car, the headache was gone. I wasn't even sure I had a head.

It had been close to an hour since Gamba called my apartment. Long enough. I headed for his place at the Royal Palms Apartments.

I took side streets. Every car was a police cruiser, now. I wasn't sure whether or not I liked the feeling that went with that.

ELEVEN

The fat young man lifted one bare foot into his lap and carefully inspected a bulbous big toe. The foot was grimed with dirt. He probed, caught something between his fingernails, yanked, and sighed.

"Durned sand-spurs," he said. "Comes of trying to keep your feet healthy."

"How's that?" I said.

"Don't wear shoes. You want healthy feet, don't ever wear no shoes. You should know that."

"I see." He had a face like a white balloon. The eyes and mouth looked painted on the rubbery surface. He was seated in a straight-backed cane-bottomed chair, leaning back against the office outside wall. Above his head a weathered black-and white-leathered sign read: The Royal Palms Apartment. A goose-neck lamp gleamed dazzling bright over the sign. Beetles, moths, and strange insects performed a shimmering circular suicide dance around the light. They rained down.

He said, "Sho, now — they're fungus to reckon with. Gits 'tween your toes. Onc't in a while a hook warm. But you want healthy feet, keep them shoes off."

"I'll remember that," I said. "I'm looking for a friend. He's renting one of your cabins. Name's Gamba. Could you tell me the number?"

"What for?" he said.

"I'd like to see him," I said.

He said, "Number Ten's the one you want."

"Thanks."

"He ain't there."

I turned back and looked at him. "How do you know?"

"He drives a bran' new Chevy station wagon, don't he? Sure he does. Well, I saw it go out a while back."

"How long a while back?"

"Not long a while."

"He was driving?"

"It's his car, ain't it?"

I didn't say anything. The bugs swirled and fell like sparse snowflakes.

"Lickety-split, he went."

"Okay," I said. *"Okay!"* We watched each other. He looked as if I'd hurt his feelings. "I'll go back and wait for him," I said. "Do you mind?"

I went to the car, got behind the wheel, and drove past the office along a shell drive among dense trees. In the rear view mirror I saw the fat young man thumb his nose at me.

Number Ten was the end cabin down by Boca Ciega Bay. Trees and shrubbery were thick around all the cabins. Most of the cars parked beside the cabins were locally licensed. Jump trade.

I clumped up the front steps of Number Ten and knocked on the door. I felt good and planned to keep a stock of those big yellow pills handy.

No sound of footsteps. Nothing. Like an empty house. The serene bayside stillness, suddenly immune to the sounds of crickets, jumping mullet, and bedsprings. Not even a bedspring from Number Ten. Nothing at all.

Passed out. Or gone in his car.

I knocked again, then tried the door. It was locked. I left the porch, walked around the side of the cabin. Lights were on inside, but I couldn't see through the windows because the blinds were drawn.

There was no grass behind Number Ten. I walked without sound on wet, hard-packed earth, through gentle winds of silence. A sleepy heron stood on the beach, staring out across black, oily water at a red blinker.

On the back porch, I side-stepped a case of bottles and reached the door. A dim light reflected against inside blinds. I tried the knob. The door was unlocked and I began to smell something.

I flung the door open and stepped into a wall of gas thick enough to stop bullets.

I held my breath, tore into the kitchen like a maniac. Light from a hallway showed a stove. Gamba was sitting on a chair in front of the stove with his head in the oven.

TWELVE

Futility struck dainty little chimes over my head.

I turned off the gas. I grabbed him, dragged him across the floor onto the porch. Bottles clattered. I pitched him down the porch steps and stretched him in the yard, then began artificial respiration. I gulped at the humid night air and knew damned well I was working on a corpse.

"You son of a bitch," I said. "You son of a bitch, breathe. Breathe."

He didn't want to breathe. After fifteen minutes, I was positive why. He might have had something he wanted to tell me. He would never tell anybody anything. He was getting colder by the second.

He was dead.

The heron flapped its wings and drifted lazily, like a lost soul, out across the bay, lifting into the night, heading for the red blinker.

I stood up. I went into the house, holding my breath, and flung all windows open. The gas began to dissipate.

I went out on the front porch and down the steps.

There was no sign of anybody. I gulped air and felt lousy. I went on out back to where he lay, cursing softly. I rolled him over. He hadn't changed. I grabbed him under the arms and lugged him back up the porch steps, across the clattering bottles and into the kitchen.

The air inside was all right now. I switched on an overhead neon, stood there and looked at him.

Vince Gamba was a lost cause.

I checked the position of the death chair. It looked as if he'd made himself comfortable, drawn the chair close to the oven, and bent the oven door down so it wouldn't be in the way. The bottom of the oven was covered with a bright canary-yellow pillow with gold fringe. He had slumped on the chair, crossed his arms inside the oven, and laid his head down. Then the gas had been turned on.

A typical suicide, somebody might say. I didn't believe it for a minute. He had known something. He had wanted to spill what he knew. He had died for it.

His face was an ugly color, choked; the eyes bulged. The flesh was evil-looking from gas death. I knelt down and went through his pockets. Sometimes they leave notes. Often, in fact. They feel they have to go out with a flourish, never thinking it's false. There was a wallet, with his name: Vincent Gamba. No address. No sign of where he worked. Something crinkled. I hauled a newly folded blue envelope from his left pants pocket. It was addressed to him at the Royal Palms Apartments. I took out the letter. It was on blue paper, written with a feminine hand in black ink:

"Dearest Vince,

I am so glad you understand the situation. We must be adult about this. Carl would never give me a divorce. So when I come back home, please don't try to see me. Everything is over, and it's much better this way. I'm returning to Carl, as his wife. A great deal of everything is my fault. I talked with him on the telephone and told him everything. He's terribly angry, but he does not blame either of us. His rage, I believe, is directed toward his own mistakes. I'm going to try to help him, and perhaps in this way right some of my own wrongs. I'm not being noble. I'm simply trying to do what I believe is right. So, Vince, you go back on the road, and sell your books and things, and become a good salesman, and make lots of money, and marry some sweet girl somewhere. Forget me — but remember my love.

Ivor."

The envelope was postmarked Orlando, Florida.

I refolded the letter slowly and placed it inside the envelope slowly, and folded that on the exact same crease, and put it back in his pocket. I stood up slowly and looked down at him.

Gassed to death.

I felt strangely dissatisfied and relentless.

I turned away and began checking Cabin Number Ten.

The living room was furnished with old rattan and a grass rug, a small bookcase full of Zane Grey, H. G.

Wells, *Marvels of the World, in Ten Volumes*, Kathleen Norris, and a bunch of dog-eared *Popular Mechanics* magazines, a couple of confession magazines, and one slim pamphlet on birth control. The room looked unlived-in. The odor of gas still lived in the softly twitching cheap curtains.

I went into the bedroom and turned on the light. The room was painted a raw blue — walls and ceiling. A naked electric bulb glared from the center of the ceiling. The floor was painted brown, flaked from hard heels. A raw red bureau, with one drawer hanging out like a sick tongue, stood to the left beside an archway that led into the living room. A ratty pink circular rug, looking as if it had been woven from old feminine underwear, was nailed to the floor by the bed. It had been torn from two of the nails. There was a red desk next to the bureau, with a sheet of paper on it and a pencil on the floor. The bed was a mess, with a clean sand-colored spread roped around the foot. An empty fifth of Gordon's Gin was on the bed. That bed had been through hell.

At the desk, I looked down on bold, heavy, male handwriting:

> *"Ivor — I cannot live without you. I don't give a damn about what you think you think, you know what I told you. You have got to listen to me — you have got to! It's wrong and you know it's wrong. Can't you see? Don't you realize that...."*

He had gouged the rest of it with the pencil until the lead broke. Between the wall and the desk was a small waste-paper basket. I looked at the wadded sheets in it. They were covered with the same blaring nothing, written in some kind of a frenzy. Drunk, maybe. Maybe he decided suicide was the only way.

I stared at the sheet of paper on the desk. Something glinted in a partly open desk drawer. I slid the drawer open, reached in and brought out a .32 automatic. I stood there looking at it. It was a Savage. I started to smell it and heard a car purr along the shell and grind to a stop.

I made it fast to the living room and looked out a window. Ivor Hendrix was paying off the driver of a yellow cab. The cab spurted off along the shell, and she turned, stumbling, toward the cabin.

She was so drunk she took the top three steps on her hands and knees.

THIRTEEN

She got to her feet on the porch and moved toward the door.

"Vince," she called softly. "Vince?"

I put the .32 automatic in my pocket, walked over to the front door, unlatched and opened it.

She stared at me, huddled against the door jamb. She looked very unhappy. She wore a thin cotton sheath dress and black pumps. The thick auburn hair was snarled. She carried the white cylindrical purse.

"You," she said. "I promised you."

She began to slide down the door jamb. I reached out, caught her arm, hauled her inside, and closed the door.

Her eyes roved the room.

"Vince," she said. "Vince."

She looked as if she had tried to fix herself up before she came to see him. The dress fit her very tightly and was as smooth as skin. Then I noticed she only had on one shoe.

"You've lost a shoe," I said.

"I'm sorry," she said, looking at me. "I promised you, and I'm sorry. I had to see him." Her eyes were like buckshot in one of these games you used to find in Cracker Jack boxes, rolling loosely, trying to find home. She was crocked to the hairline. "I sat there," she said. "I waited. There was a fifth o' wishkey in frigerdar-er-ater."

I put one arm around her slim waist and led her toward the kitchen. She began to move her lips around the name, "Vince," without speaking. She dropped her purse.

"What's happening?" she said.

"A little bit of everything, I'm afraid."

"You mad at me?"

"Yes."

"I sorry."

We reached the kitchen. I held her steady as we both looked at the body of Vince Gamba.

She shuddered and said softly, "He's dead."

I didn't say anything.

She twisted and writhed in my arms. Small cries of fright were muted in her throat, and fright ruthlessly changed her expression. Her mouth was red confusion. Facing me, she fought to break free.

I tried to keep from feeling sorry for her. She was drunk, wishing she could be sober. It wouldn't work.

"How did he die?" she gasped.

"He was murdered," I said. There was no sense in trying to explain right then. I told her, anyway — how he had phoned me, that he had been drunker than she was. "Somebody found him lying passed out on the floor. They fixed a suicide picture; stuck his head in the oven and turned on the gas. His car was seen leaving the grounds not too long ago."

She stilled. Her eyes seemed to clear somewhat.

"Why did you come here?" I said.

"You told me Vince was looking for me." Her words were clearer. She was far from sober, but the shock of seeing Gamba had evidently touched her emotions harshly enough to bring her partially around. "I knew it must have been something serious." She leaned back against my arms, her head wobbling. "I kep' drinking. I don't drink much, as a rule. Suppose that's why I finally came here. What you tol' me — it kept working on me. Vince and I agreed not to see each other."

Her gaze crept around toward the body. Abruptly, she wrenched free and veered down the hall, thumping on the one bare foot. I walked after her. She entered the bedroom, sprawled backwards across the bed.

"What'm I going to do?" she whispered. She tried to lift her head without success. "Maybe it's an accident — maybe he did it himself — maybe he...."

I said, "No. He knew something hot. He wanted to tell me. He was a serious guy, not the type to take his own life. You'll realize that when you sober up and think about it. He was too damned serious. It cost him his life. It's an old workhorse with a long gray beard, honey, but he knew something somebody couldn't afford to let anybody else know." I went over by the bed and looked down at her. "I read a letter you wrote to him, telling him it was all off."

"I never loved him," she said. "He couldn't understand that. He kept telling me he'd never b'lieve it."

"Your letter sounded as if you had cared plenty."

She closed her eyes, lying motionless. "You don't go around trying to hurt people," she said. "I wanted to let him down easy." Her eyes snapped open. "All right," she said. "I'm no good — say it. Say it!"

"Take it easy," I said.

The sheath dress was very tight. The skirt was twisted up across her soft thighs, and her small belly moved with her emotions. She arched her head back, her hands shoving up against the full thrust of her breasts. You could see how she was fighting inside, wanting to cry but not letting herself; trying to find a way out but discovering only solid black walls on every side. Trapped in the mind. Enclosed in a maze with no way out. Blaming herself.

I sat on the bed beside her.

"Easy, now," I said, feeling helpless.

She rolled suddenly toward me, flung her arms around me, her face burrowed into my chest. Her body lay pressed against me, her fingers biting into me. Her voice was small, lost, afraid. "Help me."

I laid her back on the bed, leaned above her face. Her eyes watched me with the fright like tiny flames in the deep pupils. What the hell can you tell them when they're on a spot like this? From the outside, she was a lush piece of sex, lying sprawled across a bed. Only inside, she was a frightened human being, clawing at high smooth black walls, fighting for control.

"It's rough," I said. "This does put you on a spot, but we'll see what we can do. Maybe it's going to help. Getting drunk won't help. Try to hang on, will you?"

Her fingers tightened on my arms. She watched me. The red lips parted and she breathed hot and not at all unpleasant whisky fumes into my face. "All right," she said softly. "I'll try. But help me. I'm scared. I don't know what to do. It's Carl — it must be Carl."

"Maybe," I said. "In fact, probably. But not for the reason you think." I looked down at her. The face composed itself and the red mouth smiled hesitantly. The breasts swelled as she took a long breath.

"I like you, Lee. I like you an awfully lot."

I patted her with my left hand. My palm patted bare flesh where the dress had twisted up to her hip. She didn't move. I did, damned quickly. I stood up beside the bed with my heart socking my ribs. She lay there on her back, looking up at me with a faintly cockeyed smile. Drunk, she'd forgotten everything; the dead man, the works.

"Don't go," she whispered. "I need you. Please stay for a while."

"You're tight as a coot," I said. "I almost forgot."

"Forgot what?"

"That you're drunk."

Her moment of clarity had come and gone. The fog

was in her eyes again. Her tongue was thick.

She patted the bed. "Lie down here — I wan' tell you something."

Something rattled from the back of the house. I turned quickly and headed for the kitchen. Her white purse was on the floor in the hall. I heard her moving on the bed. The bottles rattled again out there. My insides crawled and I went to the door, flung it open. A man leaped off the steps, running. I got out there. It was balloon-boy, lumbering through the dark toward the office. He would yell if I grabbed him.

I went back inside, stepped over Gamba's body, and started for the bedroom. The white purse was gone from the hall. She was on the floor in the bedroom doorway, the purse in her lap, a bottle in her hand. She took another long pull, then held the bottle upside down, her eyes gone.

"Empty," she said clearly. As I started for her, she passed out with a soft moan.

I hauled her to her feet, picked up her purse. I slung her into a fireman's carry, rammed her left arm around and caught it with my right hand. She slobbered something against my neck.

Out by the car, I draped her across the seat and shoved her over. She slumped with her long legs awry. I got behind the wheel.

The office was dark as I drove past. He would be in there, watching. On the telephone.

It was too far to take her clear across town to the motel where she was staying. Too many questions would be asked, and I couldn't answer them. I headed for her sister's house.

She was talking to me, but neither of us would ever know what she said.

FOURTEEN

"What are you trying to say?"

Asa Crafford stood in the doorway, scowling. She wore a filmy black shorty nightgown with huge red bows at the hips. It didn't look slept in and she didn't look sleepy. A light glowed behind her in the hallway, but otherwise the house was dark. I held Ivor Hendrix on her feet at my side. She kept nodding in agreement with what I said.

"I don't have time to explain," I said. "You'll just have to forget your feelings for a while. I want you to take care of your sister. She's plastered."

Asa Crafford looked disdainfully at her sister, and flipped the long fold of black hair away from her cheek. Then she looked at me.

"Is this your doing?"

"You know better than that."

"Do I?"

I walked Ivor up to her. "Take her," I said. "I don't have time to argue. She has no place to go right now. She needs help."

Ivor Hendrix nodded, her eyes half closed.

Her sister did not move, except to breathe. Then she said, "What've you been doing to her?"

"Nothing."

"You expect me to believe that? Look at her."

I looked at Asa Crafford. "Where's your husband?"

"In bed."

"Well, I'll get him the hell out of bed, if you don't hurry up and help."

She laughed through her nose. "He'd be a great help, he would. He'd just love this."

I didn't say anything. I moved Ivor Hendrix into her sister's arms. "Like I said," I told her, "I don't have time to argue now."

"You come back here!"

I started down off the porch, turned and looked at them. Asa Crafford had her arms full.

I said, "Put her to bed. Is that too much to ask?"

"Is that where you put her?"

I went down into the drive and over to the car.

"Damn you," Asa Crafford called. "Didn't you hear me?"

I got in under the wheel, slammed the door, and drove away.

I suddenly felt dead tired as I hit the street. My head was beginning to ache dully again. I stopped at the first public phone booth I saw and called Hoagy Stills again.

His wife came on. I told her I was sorry about what had happened before. She sulked and said Hoagy was getting ready to go on duty now. Finally she agreed to let him come to the phone.

"You sure have protection," I said.

"Okay. What is it now?"

I told him about the .32 automatic, but not *where* I'd found it. "Wondered if you'd run a check on it for me? It's been fired and it hasn't been cleaned."

"I see," Hoagy said.

"Can I catch you before you go on?"

"I'm just leaving."

"Hang on and I'll be right over."

"A .32, you said?"

"Right. Will you wait?"

"Look, Lee. I'm late, now. I haven't slept." He cleared his throat. "Why not come down to the lab?"

I hesitated. "Rather see you before you go on. I'm not fixed for much time."

He finally agreed. I drove to his address on Palmetto Court. He lived in a small stucco house with aluminum awnings, and a front lawn that badly needed mowing. His car, an old Packard, was parked in the drive. The porch light was on, and he was standing behind the screen door.

"Be quiet," he said. "Janie's in bed, trying to sleep." He stepped onto the porch, looked at me, and frowned. He stood five-six, heavy-set, with a face like a side of beef, small-featured. Behind the tiny blue eyes was a quick brain that had made him one of the best ballistics men anywhere. He wore a short-sleeved white sports shirt, and looked fresh-shaved and showered and as if he'd just got out of bed. "Now, what's all this about?" he said.

"I can't tell you what it's about. Not right now."

"Why not?"

"I just can't."

He looked at me. "What's this about a gun?"

I hauled out the automatic. "Thought maybe you'd check this out for me."

"Like how, for instance?"

"You know your job."

"Where'd you come by it?"

"I'd rather not say — not right now, Hoagy."

He stared at me, blinking quietly.

"Who's to know?" I said.

"I can't go around — " he said.

"All I want you to do is see if you can run down the owner of this gun, find out anything else you can. It's a long shot. You've pulled things out of the hat before."

"A long shot how, for instance?"

"Come on, Hoagy."

"Let's have it."

I gave him the gun. He looked at it, checked the clip. "Two left," he said. "Hasn't been fired in quite a time, Lee."

"But it *has* been fired."

"What's it have to do with?"

"Just do me a favor, will you, man? For cripes' sake, check it out against whatever you have, will you? Stolen guns, give it the works."

"Why not come down to the lab? I'm on duty all alone. The place is dead."

"I'd like nothing better. I can't."

"Will you give me a tip what it's all about?"

"No."

He frowned again. He took the clip out, walked to the porch light, and worked the action. "Somebody's tried to file off the serial numbers," he said. "That much'll be a cinch." He snapped the slide, rammed the clip in, dropped the gun into his pocket. "Does Haddock know?"

"No."

"There are lots of guns," he said. "What makes you

think this is special?”

"Either you will or you won't. Which is it?”

"Where can I reach you?”

"Home phone." I gave him the number. "If I'm not there, keep trying. Maybe it's nothing, but I've got a bug.”

"You telling me.”

"Thanks, Hoagy.”

"Have to do with what you asked before?”

I didn't say anything.

"Okay," he said. "But we've got boxes of guns down there, Lee." He shook his head.

I thanked him again and left.

I headed for home. The police would have to be notified about Vince Gamba's death. That would be interesting.

I parked the car and went upstairs. There were two of them standing in the hall, lounging by my door. I wouldn't have to telephone them.

"We been waiting quite a while, Baron," one of them said. "We didn't want to go in till you got here.”

FIFTEEN

I had never seen them before.

We went inside. They stood looking uncomfortable as I lit a couple of lights. I took my jacket off and hung it over the back of a chair.

"Been damp out," one said.

"Probably because it's been raining," I said.

"Yeah." He was tall, sandy-haired, wearing a hard-cloth gray suit and a dark blue tie. His eyes seemed to grin, but it was probably strain caused by staring at people. The other one was short, wiry-looking, with a black-haired crew cut. He carried a light tan jacket over one arm. His short-sleeved yellow sports shirt was buttoned without a tie at the neck.

The tall one said, "I'm Rudy Vagas, and this is Lew Steifer. Haddock thought we should drop around."

"I see," I said. "Take a load off."

They looked around the room, stiffly. Vagas sat in the center of the couch, balancing his tall frame on the edge. His gray jacket ballooned open and I saw the shoulder harness.

Steifer said, "I'll stand up, I guess. I'm sore from sitting in the car all day." He shot Vagas a quick glance. He wore his gun in a small black leather holster on his belt, left side. The grips were black. It was very neat. Everything about Steifer was neat.

"Well," I said. I turned the chair around from the big window overlooking the bay, sat down, put my ankle on my knee and jiggled my foot. "Care for a drink?"

Steifer said, "Not now. Thanks." His face suddenly became embarrassed. He was about to speak. He said, "You know we were here before, don't you. You were in here. You turned off the lights and beat it through the service door."

"I wasn't sure who it was," I said. "I didn't want to see anybody just then. There was something I had to take care of."

Vagas began to hum softly. He cracked his knuckles, looked astonished, then laughed quietly.

"All right," I said. "I wish you were here on a social

call, just to meet me, maybe. But I know it's not that. Shall we begin?"

Vagas looked at me from the couch. "Mind if I smoke?"

"Smoke."

He brought out a stubby black pipe, loaded it from a crumpled wad of lead foil that had probably once been a package of tobacco, and lit up.

Nobody spoke. Everybody was waiting.

Finally, Vagas cleared his throat. He was about forty-two and in charge. "Well, we'd like you to tell us all you know about this Carl Hendrix business, Baron."

"I don't know very much."

"You know one hell of a lot more than we do."

I shook my head. "I'm afraid not. We probably know the same things. Give me a day or two."

Vagas chewed his pipestem. "Everybody's irritated."

"Why should they be irritated?"

Steifer got that embarrassed look again and broke in fast and faintly nasty. "Because," he said, "we went out there. Even Haddock, he went. I don't understand your type of humor, Baron. I don't think anybody does."

"I don't get you," I said.

"What he means," Vagas said, "is there's no body. The lock you spoke of was busted. We looked around, but there was no dead body. We can't even be certain of the smell. It could of been a dead rat or something."

"You're kidding." I knew they weren't.

"Wish we were," Vagas said. He clacked his pipestem up and down against his teeth. "We searched out there. Didn't find a thing. Except somebody's been living in that trailer recently. And there's a fresh hole in the roof — looks like it might've been a shotgun. Or maybe the dead man who wasn't there blew his top." He did not laugh or even smile.

My mouth was open. I closed it and said, "He was there."

"All right. I believe you. Lew, here, thinks you're one of these California cowboys trying to play a practical joke of some sort to grab space in the newspapers. I'm trying to level with you. I don't go along with that. I knew your father pretty well. He was...."

"Let's leave him out of this, if it's all right with you?" I said. "It's me we're concerned with."

Vagas lifted his eyebrows and didn't lower them.

I said as frankly as I knew how, "Didn't you find anything at all?"

Steifer came in fast. "You know we didn't."

Vagas stared at me. "What did we miss?" he said.

Steifer turned to him, frowned, and looked pained at some gross stupidity on his own part. He had flubbed. It was terribly important that he had flubbed, and he wouldn't forget it for three days.

"The body was in the cement block house," I said.

Vagas shook his head, tamped his pipe, relit it.

"Was the trailer open?"

"Yes."

"Was there a bottle of Old Overholt on the drainboard?"

Vagas said, "No. I saw it outside, though — empty."

"I picked it up and looked at it," Steifer said. "Like Rudy says, it was empty."

"Now that we've solved that mystery," Vagas said. "Let's draw some specific word pictures." He cleared his throat. "Sheriff Silverman is hot — you should of called him, you know that. It's under his jurisdiction. Anyway — Chief Garlik's hot. Haddock's hot." He turned to Steifer. "Who isn't hot?"

Steifer said, "I don't know."

Vagas stared at him, then looked at me. "Lew's wife's having a baby," he said.

"That probably accounts for it," I said. "If it's Silverman's territory, how come you guys are here?"

"There's an agreement," Vagas said. He looked vaguely at his pipe. "We know you're just starting in business here, Baron. We know it can be tough. So, all right. Everybody's friendly. We're all willing to help each other, and if you'll just help us, everything'll work just fine."

"The hell with it, Rudy," Steifer said.

"No," Vagas said. "He's got to understand. He's causing confusion without meaning to." He looked at me. "We know you been buzzing around all afternoon and evening. Right? We don't know what it's all about. You reported a dead body. I think there was a dead body. But you're holding out on us — you've got to be." He hesitated. "Look at it this way. You're a stranger. In a section you don't know anything about. And right away, trouble."

"I haven't had a chance to talk with you. I told Lowell I wasn't holding out on you. I said I'd tell him everything I knew." I paused. "I have a client, and it's a sort of missing person deal."

"All right. Did you check with the bureau?"

I sighed. "No."

"There you are." His expression became serious. "I'm

not trying to be funny, trying to gouge you. Hell, I even thought of setting up my own agency here, once. It could be a good deal. Especially good right here, the way things are getting. It's ripe for the kind of business you're in. Good Christ, we can work together. It's done all the time."

"Sometimes," I said. "And other times, a client expects certain things of you. Without such trust, where would I be? The only publicity a guy like myself gets is word of mouth. You make somebody happy, and he tells somebody else. Maybe it's only finding a stolen dog...."

"Or maybe something more than that?" Vagas said. He kept on looking at me with his eyebrows hooked up "Detectives get shot, too, don't you see? Or their licenses get taken away. Know something? There was a guy here last summer, from some place in the Midwest. He opened an agency. A real sharpie, and he got off on the wrong foot."

"Who's that?" Steifer said.

"Blakely," Vagas said. "Ned Blakely, remember? Well," he went on, "Blakely was on something and he knew it. We had two men on him night and day. But, like I say, he was sharp. He gave them the slip. Next morning, he was washed up against the sea wall out to Maderia Beach. His throat was cut from here to here. He hadn't leveled with us — wouldn't tell us a thing." He shrugged. "It's unsolved, a dead issue. We never got a thing to go on."

"So I'm a sharpie?"

"I mean we could've helped him. If he'd just told us something."

"Maybe he couldn't tell you," I said. "Ever think of

that? Since when do you read minds? Maybe he was in a tight."

"What are the police for?" Vagas said.

"Your old man played it smart," Steifer said.

"All right," I said. "Push me. My old man was a lummox. He was a great guy, but he believed the book. Sometimes the book isn't right. You go through life believing every word in the book, that's all right. You live it your way. It's not my way." I stopped talking, and they didn't speak. I said, "It's not that I don't want to come to you. You have facilities, means of operations I'll never have. But I can't *always* come to you."

"James Baron came to us."

"You're speaking of two different people."

"He stayed in business," Steifer said.

"He was a flunkie," I said. "He might just as well have been in uniform. He came to you because he believed in the book. That was dandy for him, and dandy for you, in case he ever bumped into anything. It made your job easier. You liked him for it, like hell you did — and that made him happy, like hell it did. Anyway, even if you both were happy, I can exist without having you like me. And, by the way, nobody's taking away my license without good reason."

"You plan on staying in business here?"

"That's right."

"Maybe he *wants* to be sharp," Steifer said.

"I want to be good at my business," I said. "That's straight from the cornfields, but it's still true. It's all I want, right now. Someday I'd like to have a wife and family. Not for a while. I appreciate what you're saying."

"Your father made his business pay."

"Made it pay? I guess maybe you didn't know him, after all. You can follow the whole thing on his records. Your names are on them, I saw them. With pen and ink, he was a hot baby. He was interested in everything you guys did, along with everything else. But the minute he walked out of that office door, he was sunk. He had no business. You can see it die, from twenty-five years back. Because word got around, the way it does. If you were in bad trouble, he wasn't the guy to see. He played with you guys, see? Listen, there are people who need help. They're strapped to a rack. They've given up fighting, or they can't fight any more. They come to me. They're my clients. I'm keeping it that way."

"That's it, then," Vagas said.

"Not quite," I said. "You know how I feel. On the other hand, I told Lowell I wasn't going to keep anything from him. That's not the idea."

Vagas held his pipe with both hands and shook his head. "I don't get you."

Steifer made a noise in his throat.

I said, "Are you up to date on this Laketown bank robbery?"

Vagas' voice was hollow. "How?"

Steifer didn't move.

I said, "I don't think the body I found was Carl Hendrix. I think it was Barton Yonkers, the bird that escaped from Raiford recently. I think he robbed the Laketown Union Trust, and I think he came down here with the money and somebody knocked him off for it."

"Jesus Christ!" Steifer said. "Jesus Christ, Rudy!"

Vagas turned his head slowly and looked at Steifer. Then he looked at me, the eyes grinning. "Why?" he said.

"It's interesting, isn't it? Okay, first, the body of the man I found had no arms, his face had been chopped with a hatchet. Somebody had tried to cut his head off, but they either didn't have the stomach for it, or they didn't have time. Time definitely is an element in this thing — or it was."

"How do you mean, 'was'?"

"I'll get to that."

Steifer said, "He'll get to that. Jesus Christ, Rudy — we'd better take him downtown."

Vagas didn't even bother looking at him this time.

I said, "Sure, it sounds fantastic. Whoever got that Laketown loot should have taken off for Paris or someplace. Only they didn't. Something happened and fouled the whole thing up."

Steifer was so nervous he was practically dancing standing still. Vagas was excited, too, but it only showed deep in his eyes and in the knuckles of the hand that held the black pipe.

I said, "There might be a reward, since it's a bank deal. Now, look — a Mrs. Johnson was in the Union Trust at the time of the robbery. She said she saw one of the two men who held the place up, and that he carried a suitcase with the initials 'K. S. L.' on it. I found the suitcase. It's out behind that trailer, in a trash pit, half burned."

Vagas held up his hand. "What put you on this?"

I told him about the paper currency band.

"The floor was bare when we looked," he said.

"Somebody got wise, went back there and got rid of the body," I said. "Along with anything they might have left laying around, overlooked — because of haste."

"How did they get wise?" Vagas said. He didn't wait for me to answer. "I'll tell you: because you tipped him, somehow. You," he said. "What I been trying to get across."

"Yeah," Steifer said.

"Nuts," I said. "Buzzards would have found that body and cleaned the bones, before you ever got out there. This is the thanks I get."

"All right," Vagas said. "It sounds. What else?"

"What the hell else do you want?"

"You been sitting on your backside thinking about this ever since you called Haddock? Don't make me laugh in your face." Vagas edged himself half off his narrow perch on the sofa. "What leads you got? Who's suspect?"

I leaned forward. "This isn't that kind of a thing," I said. "The whole state of Florida is suspect."

"Who's Carl Hendrix?"

"I wish I knew."

"Where is he?"

"I wish I knew that. It could be he was the second man along with Yonkers on the robbery. It could be he's gone fishing for a few days."

"Who's your client?"

I had waited for that. I shook my head slowly, watching him. "Tell you something, though. I think you should pick up a guy named Joe Lager. He hangs out on First Street. I saw him in the Oriental Tavern."

"Lager," Vagas said. "We know him."

"What on?"

"Petty thief. Last thing, he was growing weed in three of his friends' garages, in coffee cans. Okay, we pick him up. What we ask him?"

"That's up to you," I said.

"What else?" Vagas said. He was thinking. He stared at me, but his eyes were veiled. He was reading something interesting in the back of his head. He said, "Carl Hendrix's wife, right?"

"Carl Hendrix's wife right what?"

"Your client. What got you on this."

I grinned at him. It was a stiff and unlikely grin. "Come now," I said. "You'll have to do better than that."

"Don't try to snow me, Baron," Vagas said. "All it takes is a little reasoning. You've avoided the wife as if she doesn't exist, and all the time she's as obvious as a fire would be under your chair."

I just spoke without thinking, trying to think behind the speaking, "Maybe he hasn't got a wife, ever consider that?"

Vagas started to say something and the phone rang. I came out of my chair like a shot, reaching. Steifer leaned and picked up the phone. He chatted for a moment, then began to look like a fish-stuffed cat, clamped the phone in its cradle, looked at Vagas. "All right," Vagas said. "What is it?" Steifer gloated sickeningly. He turned to me and said, "How did you happen along to turn off the gas?"

Vagas' voice was like ice in bed against your back.

"What is it, Lew?"

The fish-stuffed cat had caught a big fat mouse. But the cat wasn't hungry. He would play with the mouse, and nothing would distract him. "Name's Vincent Gamba," Steifer said. "A salesman of cookingware, religious periodicals, pamphlets on birth control that he authored himself, phony wedding and engagement rings. Also believed to have a sideline in rubber goods and etceteras, because the stock found would break a horse's back if — "

"Get with it, Lew."

"Dead," Steifer said. "Of having his head in an oven with the gas turned on. Doc Salters claims the guy was so drunk that if he got his head stuck in the oven, he'd never be able to get it out." He looked at me. "Witness saw Lee Baron present on spot around time of death. Witness took Baron's license number as he sped off premises."

He hadn't mentioned seeing Ivor Hendrix. I said, "Will it do me any good to say I planned telling you about this?"

"I don't think so," Vagas said. "It might."

"I just hadn't got to it yet."

Steifer said, "There's more. A bit of mystery added. The witness claims he saw Gamba leave the motel a while before Baron came. Gamba was driving his new Chevrolet station wagon like a crazy man. The station wagon did not return."

Vagas looked at me. I told them everything I knew about Vince Gamba from the moment he held me up with the shotgun in the trailer, accounting for the hole in the trailer roof. I said nothing of Ivor Hendrix or the Craffords. I knew Vagas was thinking. I said, "Gamba called me here. He was plastered. He said he had to see me, and he raved about buried money, but wouldn't tell me anything till I came and talked with him. That's when you birds were outside the door. Now you know why I didn't want to hang around."

"Okay," Vagas said. He knocked his pipe out in an ash tray and stood up. "It could've been nice if you'd told us all this a few hours ago." He blinked sleepily. "At least one life would have been saved."

I said nothing.

"We would've picked this Gamba up. He would've been in a cell, sobering up, awaiting questioning."

The phone rang. This time I nailed it and showed Steifer my teeth. I felt sick about the way things were going. It was Hoagy Stills, calling from the lab. Maybe he had something on the .32 automatic I'd given him.

"Minute I tell you what I've got," he said, "I'm going to Garlik with it. He'll see Haddock. I'm going to tell them I told you."

"All right."

Hoagy was mad. I looked at Vagas and Steifer. They watched me. I began to perspire.

"Slugs fired from the .32 automatic you gave me were found in the dead body of a teller killed in that Laketown bank robbery you're interested in. The teller's name was McCarthy."

"How did you run that down?"

"Enlarged photostats of the slugs in McCarthy. They were sent to every department in the state of Florida for ballistics checks against .32's on hand. It socked me in the eye. You know what this means."

"Yes."

"All right. After I tell Haddock, they'll have orders to pick you up. I'll tell them where I spoke to you. They'll flay my hide and rub it with salt. Jesus Christ. Can I say you gave me your word you wouldn't leave town?"

I felt like absolute hell. Hoagy was out on a limb for me and I was going to saw the limb off. "Yes."

"This is lousy, Lee, lousy. It'll rip the whole state wide open. This area will be crawling. They'll get you, and Christ knows what they'll do to you. They're rough here, Lee. Things have changed in the past ten years. They play it hard. They'll smash you — they'll run you out of town, if you survive. Goddamn it. Only reason I've called you first's because we've been friends, and I know you don't know what this town is any more. You better find some quick answers — either that, or you're dead. What you going to do?"

"Sit down and cry," I said. "No. I don't know. But thanks, I mean that." He should have gone to Garlik first. The damned fool.

"Does it help?" Hoagy said.

"Yes."

"You can't talk," he said. He said it with care.

"No."

"Oh, Jesus." He hung up.

I hung up and stood there staring stupidly at Vagas and Steifer, feeling a stiff and insane grin on my face.

"Who was that?" Steifer said.

"Marilyn Monroe. She's leaving her husband. She just wanted to make sure I'm still waiting."

Vagas watched me. He heaved a long deep sigh. "All

right." He had a sly look about him. He was scheming something. He looked at Steifer, then at me again. "We'll want to talk with you later."

I said nothing. His nostrils turned pale and waxen.

"Come on, Ruby," Steifer said, turning toward the door. "Let's get out of here. It smells."

"Know what you just did?" Vagas said. "You ruined your chances in this town. You're done."

"How?"

"You haven't leveled with me."

He turned and they went to the door, and on out. Vagas shut the door. He shut it softly.

They would be back. Vagas was setting something up, and I couldn't figure what it was. I had missed something between him and Steifer, when I was talking with Hoagy.

How in hell could I level with them? If this thing was mine, I couldn't. Only I had to find the answers, the right answers, and quickly. I thought of Ivor Hendrix and had an immediate feeling of danger lurking around her, aimed at her. I didn't know exactly why.

I went into the bedroom. I was immediately conscious of the fact that Vagas and Steifer had searched the apartment before I survived. You put things a certain way. It takes a top cop to set them back the same, and they had muffed it. I checked the top drawer in the bureau for my 9mm Browning. It was gone. I gnawed the inside of my cheek, headed for the living room. The snapshots of Carl Hendrix were still on the table where I'd left them after talking with Ivor Hendrix. They would have seen them, but the photos wouldn't have meant anything.

At this moment everybody in the Police Building knew about the .32 Savage automatic. One or two cruisers would be within blocks of this apartment. The prowl car boys would be receiving calls.

The telephone shrilled savagely.

I went. I didn't bother to close the door.

The phone was still ringing as I started down in the elevator. I wondered if I would ever hear that same phone ring again.

Leaving the parking area, I spotted the police car on open ground, shadowed against the paler waters of Tampa Bay. I knew then what Vagas had planned. Tail me and let me do the leading.

It irritated me plenty. I turned the lights off, set the gas pedal on the floor, and lost the car in the tangle of residential streets on my way to the Crafford address.

Maybe Steifer was driving.

SIXTEEN

Asa Crafford's eyes were big and hot. She still wore the filmy black shorty nightgown with the big red bows, and she still didn't look sleepy.

"How is she?" I said.

"She's fine. She's so fine she isn't even here."

I shoved her out of the way and walked through into the hall. "Where did you have her?"

"Down there — the room off the end of the hall. Wait, Lee. I tell you she's not here."

I kept walking fast down the length of the hall. This was one great big beautiful God-damned night, this was. I reached the end of the hall. She ran along behind me. I turned into an unlighted room, found the wall switch, flipped it.

Across the room was a broad couch where somebody had been lying. A red woolen blanket was snarled off across the floor. There was a dent in a large yellow pillow where her head must have lain.

"Where is she?"

Asa Crafford eyed me, smiling. I took hold of her shoulders and shook her. Her breasts swung bobbling and her body gave sensuously with the pressure of my hands.

"I like it when you're rough," she said.

"Where is she!"

"I tried to sober her up. I let her sleep a while. Then I dragged her into the shower and turned it on full blast. She came around. I fed her black coffee, then dosed her with a Dexedrine bomb. It worked, but she wouldn't tell me anything. She just wanted to get away."

"So you let her."

"Elk took her. He was hanging around when I had her in the shower, the bastard. 'Need a towel?' he said. I left him with her. Next thing I heard was the car, and he'd taken her away. The hell with both of them, darling."

"Where would he take her?"

"How should I know?"

"This is great," I said.

"Care for a drink?"

"Yes."

She turned and walked back down the hall. I went after her. She turned into the big front room.

"I'm over here. In case you're interested."

I stood there. The room was lighted softly around the baseboards. Her legs were long and white and smooth, swelling to lush thigh and hip and the ruffle of black gown with the red bows, then the breasts, the lips, the eyes. Soft slow blue jazz flowed like warm milk through the room from a record player. I went over and flipped the record arm off, then looked at her.

She stood with her back to me at the bar, pouring things from bottles into glasses that were damned near a foot tall.

"I like that music," she said. It had been Duke Ellington's *Mood Indigo*. "It reminds me of me."

The light was arranged so you could see through the gown; the swollen curves, the way she moved.

She came over to me with the glasses in her hands. She stood with her hips thrown forward.

I took one glass and then took three long swallows, bringing the liquid down considerably. It was good. It hit bottom and began to grind. Something worked up my spine, and tiny feet pattered on the back of my skull. Then one of the feet expanded and booted me between the eyes.

"Vodka and cognac," she said. "Good, isn't it? Of course, you drink it much too fast. You're crude, Lee. You always were. But, then, that's all right, too."

I didn't say anything. Somebody had gone out there to that cement block house and jimmied the lock. They had carried the body away into the dark wet night.

Snatchers. Burke and Hare.

The day was done. The night was shot to hell. I couldn't keep my eyes off her. I thought things.

"You must have a real bad impression of me," she said.

"Depends what you mean by bad."

"Things I've said. How I've acted."

"Since when were you worried about impressions?"

She looked into her glass, then up at me. "I know how I sound," she said. Suddenly her eyes narrowed. "I don't give a damn," she said. "What the hell of it?" She tipped her glass and drank fast, gulping it.

"That'll solve everything," I said.

"I have to sneak out," she said. "Did you know that? And when I get back, you know what happens? He beats me. That's what happens." She laughed bitterly. "Isn't that swell? I rebel, but it doesn't do any good. He beats me, then he goes to the *Carol* and mopes."

"*The Carol?*"

"His boat. Oh, I hadn't told you. Oh, yes. He's a sailor, too. Named after his first wife. Know why he beats me? Because Carol would never have acted like I do."

"Why don't you leave him?"

"I'm afraid to. I'm afraid what he would do to me. He loves me, in his own insane way." She turned, moved to the bar, set her glass down, then returned to me. "God," she said. "All I need is money. You hear? Money." She formed claws with her hands, then smiled over the claws, and relaxed them, put her hands behind her. "He's spent every damned cent we had. He inherited a lot from his parents, and he's into everybody he knows. I think he's as desperate as I am. If I had the money, I'd go — oh, how I'd go, then." She paused. "I like money almost as much as I like sex. It does crazy things to me — just feeling of it." Her eyes got dreamy. "Once I kept at him till I got a thousand dollars from him. That was before he'd gone through everything. I went to the bank and cashed it all into single dollar bills. A thousand of them. It's crazy, sometimes when I think of it — but I'd do it again. I brought it all home and spread it around in my bed and slept with it." She put her hands in front of her and clenched them together. "It was wonderful." She shivered again. She looked at me, the eyes narrow and slightly drunk. "I think real crazy things," she said. "Then I sneak out — and when I come back, he beats me." She swallowed.

The telephone in the hall rang gently. She said, "Excuse me," and left the room. I started toward the hall door. I heard her speak in a rapid whisper. I went back to the bar as she hung up. She returned. I set my glass down and moved across the room.

"I'm leaving," I said.

"Lee? Come on upstairs. I mean it."

I walked fast out into the hall and down toward the front door. I looked back as I went through the door. She hadn't left the living room.

I went on outside and got into the car and sat there. I was very tired. I needed sleep, and there was no place to go. I wanted to see what happened here, if anything. I started the car and inched it around the drive into the street, then came back in the other side of the drive and pulled the car up on the lawn. I parked under some bushes that were taller than the car, climbed over into the back seat, and lay down.

I thought of them, staked out at my apartment. Hotels and motels and rooming houses would be alerted. They would cool off a little by morning. The drink had been big and powerful, and I began to doze. I had to get some sleep.

At the sound of the opening door I opened my eyes and saw her. She was naked in the night light. I didn't move.

"Lee?" she said.

She gave a kind of moan and lay down on me. I caught a glimpse of her face and it was wrung, and red-lipped, with the eyes shining. Her mouth pressed against mine. The lips were hot, the tongue probing. I rolled her over on the seat. She lay there on her back, looking at me, her lips and teeth and eyes shining. Her body was smooth and urgent against my hands. As I touched her, she breathed inward between her teeth. She spoke harshly, almost with anger. "Love me. Please, love me."

It went on for a long time. Then we would nap. Then one of us would wake up and kiss the other, and it would start all over again. She didn't seem to want to leave.

Sometime in the early morning a car stopped out front. A man went up to the door and rang the bell. I couldn't see who it was. They did not see my car. I didn't care who it was, right then.

Along about daylight, she left. She kissed me and slipped outside and closed the car door.

I watched her run naked. She held her breasts as if

they were tender, and bounded off across the dew-wet lawn through the gray light of dawn. The house door closed. It was quiet again.

A car gunned fast past the front of the house. A rolled morning newspaper flew from the driver's window, arced high, and plopped halfway up the lawn.

SEVENTEEN

I felt beat.

I was groggy and my head ached. It was badly swollen in spots, and the spots were sore to the touch. When I looked out of my eyes, it was as if I wore dark blinders at the edges. There was that tired feeling of car upholstery and dust, mingled with perfume and a lingering odor of cognac. My feet burned. I wasn't hungry, but if I didn't get some coffee down quick, I would probably just sit here for the rest of the week.

I got out of the car and walked across the lawn, picked up the newspaper, and came back. I lit a cigarette, creaked in under the steering wheel, rolled the rubber band off the paper and snapped it out into the grass. The cigarette tasted like the odor of sunburned seaweed.

At the bottom of the first page, a headline caught my eye. A new body had been found. Barton Yonkers' bank-robbing buddy. He was very, very dead.

BODY THROWS LIGHT ON
LAKETOWN BANK ROBBERY

Dead Man Discovered near Lake Wales Links Raiford Escapee with Laketown Loot

Lake Wales, (AP)—The body of a man discovered in a cypress woods near Lake Wales has been identified as that of Horace Ailings, 43, ex-convict and known criminal, wanted by police in several states. Although the body was badly decomposed, experts have been able to determine the identity through a fingerprint process. Two persons present during the Laketown bank holdup claim they recognize the clothes worn by Ailings, as well as the color of the dead man's hair.

Prison authorities revealed that shortly over a month ago, lifer-convict Barton "Duck-Eyes", "Legs", "The Gambler" Yonkers, 36, pulled a ruse and executed a spectacular escape. It was also revealed that Yonkers was a close friend of Ailings. An inmate (name withheld) claims Yonkers told him he would meet Ailings on the outside, and that they "had something lined up."

What excites police theory more is the fact that Yonkers has a large, possibly infected appendectomy scar on his abdomen.

In the warden's words: "Yonkers was smooth. He convinced prison medicos he had a ruptured appendix, faked his way to hospital, and was operated on. The operation revealed nothing wrong, but Yonkers continued to complain convincingly of bad pains. Because Yonkers seemed desperately ill, guards relaxed their vigilance. He escaped the first night after the operation, and prison doctors say he'll be in serious condition unless he's placed himself under the care of some competent underworld physician. Police theorize Yonkers immediately joined Ailings and they executed the planned robbery. It is well known that letters 'kited' into prison reach inmates without detection, and this is probably how the Laketown robbery was schemed. Police further theorize Yonkers murdered Ailings after the get-away. Medical professionals are seeking to determine how Ailings died.

"Witnesses to Laketown's Union Trust robbery back police beliefs with statements that one of the gunmen revealed obvious pain, holding his middle, limping...."

The remainder of the yarn dealt with the warden's apologies to the press for not stating how Yonkers made good his escape past bars, guards, and walls. Until plans could be made to prevent any similar future escape, this information would be withheld.

I refolded the paper, tossed it out on the lawn, started the car, and drove away from there. By now the city department, and the sheriff's department, were both concerned with my whereabouts. Doubtless every on-duty cruiser had been ordered to skip drive-in coffee breaks and be on the lookout. Vagas was wise to Ivor

Hendrix being my possible tie-in. Hoagy Stills had jeopardized his job for me.

I felt a sudden sense of guilt over not trying to locate Ivor Hendrix earlier.

I drove through morning overhang to my apartment. Crossing Fourth Street, I saw a police car headed in the opposite direction. I took the bayside road toward Bahama Shores. The sun was coming up hot and yellow over Tampa Bay.

If one of them hadn't moved to look at his wrist watch so his elbow jutted past the apartment house entrance, I would have driven by and they would have spotted me. It was Steifer's elbow, in the light-colored sports jacket. Still on duty, he would be in a rage.

I made a U-turn, parked on the shoulder beside some cabbage palms, and watched. There were three uniformed cops, Steifer, and Vagas. Probably two more upstairs, and maybe another on the rear fire escape.

I left, stopped at a grocery store with a small lunch counter. After two phone calls, I located *The Carol*, Elk Crafford's boat, at the Calcutta Shores Yacht Club. I drank two cups of coffee, ate a packaged ham sandwich that tasted as if it belonged between the leaves of an old family Bible, and drove away.

I booted the car south, avoiding cruiser routes, and stopped to waste time and have another cup of coffee in White City. I found myself staring at a phone booth with a feeling of stupidity.

I put through a long distance call to Mrs. Elizabeth Haskins, in Orlando. There was a short wait. It was getting on toward nine o'clock. Finally the operator called back with my party.

"Mrs. Elizabeth Haskins?"

"Ye-us?"

I told her my name, and said I was a friend of Carl's. "Just got into town, and remembered him mentioning your name. Wondered if you could tell me where they live? I'd like to visit them."

She gave me the Pine Park trailer address in a thick, giggly, Southern voice, full of fried yams, hammocks and honeysuckle.

"How is Carl?" I said.

"Oh, land. I haven't laid sight on Carl in some time. It must be — well, a long, long while."

"And Ivor? Still as pretty as ever?"

"Ivor? Oh, you mean his wife? My, my — I 'clare, I've never even *met* the girl. Pretty, you say? My, my — I 'clare. Do tell me about — oh, but you haven't seen them in a spell, either? I don't know what's getting into me. What did you say your name was?"

"That's all right, Mrs. Haskins. Thanks a lot."

"You just might ..."

"Yeah. That's what I figure. G'by."

I walked away. I felt a little crazy. As if somebody had bored slowly into my head with an awl, or chopped it with an adz, or whatever they use to work on old hard skulls with.

Nearly a month in Orlando with Carl's aunt.

EIGHTEEN

It was a long green Florida morning. Tampa Bay was a valley of diamonds. I drove to Calcutta Shores and argued my way past the white linen suit with the black-billed cap at the entrance gate, then tooled my bruised Stude warily into the parking area among the Continentals, Cads, and Imperials. There was no sign of copper. I saw nothing of the Crafford pink Cad.

Another linen suit skipped up to me, curtsied, and toothed brightly about free gin and dandy-fine morning pick-me-up coconut milk and brandy at the "fabulously fascinating" inside bar.

"No thanks," I said. "Just finished breakfast."

That brought an understanding wink. Was I a new member of the club? No, I wasn't. I had been invited to partake of their luxurious layout by Mr. Elk Crafford.

The linen suit flew away.

I hid the car behind a cluster of bamboo and walked down the sloped lawn.

Glittering golden masts and sails like folded napkins tilted and tipped in rhythmic counterpoint beyond the calculated carpet of trained grass and white sea wall. Slim, varnished piers, like well manicured fingers, lay in the water between rows of colorful boats; blues, greens, reds, yellows, brass and high-varnished mahogany.

Darkly tanned men and women moved with a kind of nervous earnestness among tables and beach chairs. They grinned a lot. Most of them held drinks in their hands. It was never too early.

A pretty, dark-haired girl with a coffee tan, wearing a cream swimsuit, ran up the slope. She had a sleek body, gorgeous legs, golden toenails.

"Excuse me," I said as she veered past.

She paused, raised her eyebrows, said, "Hmm-m-m?" and smiled at me. Her fingernails were golden, too, but her lips were red.

"Wonder if you know the *Carol?*"

"Oh?" She turned and looked down at the boats, then aimed her blue gaze at me. "You mean Elk's tub." She gave a crystal laugh, then said, "Over there, darling." She held her right hand close to her breast and bent her forefinger into a hook, pointing. "See?"

"Afraid not."

She moved closer with a quick glance and put her left arm around me and placed her soft right arm against my cheek, lining her finger up so I could take aim.

"You need a shave," she said. Her voice was like brandy at midnight. "Now, right there, darling. Second pier. Just past Duane's Chris-Craft. Got it now?"

I saw the *Carol*. The girl did not move her arm. Finally she did, watching me soberly.

I said, "Maybe you'll let me buy you a drink after a while — sometime." I gestured vaguely.

She smiled. Somewhere a star went out. "Sorry, darling. It's quite impossible. I'm all taken up." She turned and ran off along the slope.

I watched her. She was having trouble with her swimsuit. It only took me a minute to learn how to walk again.

The pier echoed under my feet. I passed a small, trim outboard, tied to the pier, red paint blazing in bright sunlight. Beyond the sun, the sky was a mountain range of bloated black cloud.

The *Carol* was tied bow in. Her stern was anchored diagonally out from the pier's end. A narrow gangplank was secured to the bow, moving faintly in a swell. I heard Ivor Hendrix talking from the cabin.

There was fright in her voice.

A float, loaded with piled fish net and two large barrels, swung at anchor beside the schooner. I jumped from the pier, landed on the float, knelt beside the pile of reeking net. The boat's shadow covered me.

"No," Ivor Hendrix said. "I don't want to." She paused for some time. I realized she was speaking over the telephone. Wires led to the *Carol* from a pier-box on a pole. Her tone was close to strident. "Never mind, I tell you — no."

I knelt there. I rubbed a numb spot on my forehead. The story of my life: picking up murder's refuse, like dried, bloody feathers fluttering through bright sunlight.

She said, "Vine tree?" and her voice lowered with a sly tinge. "Yes, that's all right, then. Certainly. You know me better than that. Yes, all right."

I knelt there, hidden by the barrels and the fish net, waiting. Who else was aboard with her? Elk?

I heard her hang up. Silence.

I waited.

I thought I heard her moan, very softly.

I stared into the water over the side of the float. A large, crazy-eyed fish surfaced, took one long look at me, bubbled, and dove flashing for home.

NINETEEN

I came aboard like a cat in the night. There was no sound from below.

The companionway hatch was hooked open. The *Carol* rode the swell, creaking. She was varnished, cared for, her brass glinting. An empty whisky bottle chinked back and forth in the center of rolled hawser. A gull leaned and necked and billed on a loosely swinging boom.

"Who's that?"

Her voice sounded as if somebody had a knife-tip at her belly. I waited.

"Who's there?"

Still on cat feet, like Chicago's fog, I neared the companionway. I stood so my shadow wouldn't fall below.

I could hear her breathing and peeked below. She stood three feet from the end of the steps, leaning across a bunk. She was looking out a port, one hand with the fingers clenched beside her cheek.

I grabbed the ledge atop the companionway, swung in, and dropped two feet from her. She was alone.

She whirled, slapped both hands to her face, and started to scream. She recognized me. She moved back and sat down on the bunk.

"Who was on the phone?" I said.

"Thank God, it's you."

"Who was on the phone?"

"Elk — my sister's husband. He wondered if I was

all right. I was telling him I had to leave here."

She still wore the sheath dress of the night before. It was rust-colored. She had on a pair of tan pumps. Her hair was brushed to a coppery sheen, thick and rich. She did not look hung over. She did look scared. Her eyes kept roving toward the port through which, beyond the pier, you could see the green slope of lawn, with the men and women strolling, drinking.

There was a bunk opposite hers. I sat on it and stared at her, hearing the morning silence. Her fingers betrayed her nervousness. I looked at her face, the faintly slanted eyes, the sad, frightened mouth, and some of my irritation vanished.

I said, "I just talked with Elizabeth Haskins."

"You did?"

I nodded. "She said she's never met you."

She lifted one hand slowly and covered her lips with the tips of her fingers. She shook her head, and said, "I'm sorry." She lowered the hand. "I know what you must think. I forgot to say anything about that. I'd told her to tell anyone who called that she'd never met me, that I'd never been there. It was because of Vince." She hesitated. "And I think it was a little because of Carl, too. I was afraid — I'm still more frightened now." She moved her head slowly from side to side. "I'm terribly sorry — I should have told you."

"Forget it."

"I can call her, now," she said. "You can talk with her, with me right here. She'll explain."

"Never mind. How come you're scared now? What's happened?"

The telephone was on a sunken bookshelf at the foot

of the bunk she sat on. She looked at the telephone.

"Somebody called — here. Just before I talked with Elk. It was a man. He said he was helping Carl, that Carl was in a jam, and that I knew it. He said he was coming to get me, to take me to Carl. He said Carl was fed up with what I was doing — he was going to put a stop to it, once and for all." She paused. "He was frightening."

"How."

"The way he talked."

"What'd he say Carl wanted you for?"

She stood up quickly with her hands clasped together and said in a small, tense voice that was close to hysteria, "I don't know," and sat down again.

"How would they know you're here?"

"I don't know that, either. He said it wouldn't do any good to try and hide any more."

She looked trapped and fearful.

"That all the man said?"

She nodded rapidly.

"You didn't talk with Carl? No idea where he is?"

She shook her head.

"Why did you come here with Elk?"

"I asked him to take me someplace. I was going to have him take me to the motel. Then, I don't know, it frightened me — I asked him if I could stay here on the *Carol*, for the night. He didn't ask any questions. He left me here. I slept here — I felt safer here." She stared at her hands, moved her thumbs around, then looked up at me. "I didn't want to stay in that house. She said a lot of awful things."

"I can imagine."

"I'm sorry about last night. It's — I can't explain why I did what I did. I drank too much. Then it seemed as if the only right thing to do was go see Vince, because he'd asked to see me. And then — "

"Then what?"

"You know what. You were there."

"You remember what you said when you were lying on the bed?"

She nodded. "I don't feel wrong about what I said, then."

"Have you heard anything from Carl?"

"No." She paused. "Only what I told you."

"Where did Elk go after he left you last night?"

"I have no idea. He only stayed a few minutes. I don't know where he went."

"He didn't go home."

"No? How — oh."

"How, oh, what?"

"Nothing."

"I was staked out across the street," I lied. "Waiting for you to come back."

"Did you go to my motel?"

"That's not — " I stopped talking. She was looking past my shoulder as she spoke.

"There's a policeman out there."

I turned and glanced through the port. Beyond the pier, a police cruiser had parked by the edge of the green lawn. The morning was gray now, the sun was gone. Two harness cops were talking with the man on the lawn. They had obviously traced Crafford through Hendrix's name, made a routine check at the Calcutta Shores Yacht Club, and discovered my car. It would be that simple.

I turned back to Ivor Hendrix, quickly explained the situation. "If they get me now, I'm finished in this town," I told her. "Done. I won't stand a chance because I can't come up with anything yet. I don't know any answers. They're ready to finish me off. If they get you, I won't be able to help you. Christ knows how long they'll hold you, what you'll have to go through. I'm not sure how they operate here. I have an idea, and it's not good. It's up to you. I've got to run for it — somehow. Will you chance it with me?"

For a moment she couldn't speak. I knew I'd have to do the best I could, try to find out anything else I could, and lay the whole mess on Haddock's desk, and hope for the best. There was no other way.

She would have to come with me.

"There's an outboard a few feet down the pier," I said. "We might stand a chance. They're looking for me, not you. If we walk quietly — and together — we might make it."

"I don't want to stay here. I'm frightened sick of Carl."

I shoved her ahead of me. We came out on the deck. One of the harness bulls was standing by the clubhouse door. They still weren't wise to the *Carol*. Another cruiser turned into the parking area. They had the bit on the radio already. Then I saw the girl in the cream-colored swimsuit walking slowly across the lawn toward the cops. She would spill fast.

We came off the gangplank and down to the pier. I felt Ivor Hendrix stiffen.

"My purse," she said. "I've got to go back. I forgot it."

"There's no time."

"I want it."

She twisted free and ran up the gangplank, the tight skirt of the sheath dress snagging in the hollows of her knees, her firm round hips undulant. I shot a look over at the lawn. The cops still weren't coming this way. I could feel my heart rock. I went back aboard the *Carol*, taking the gangplank in two strides. She had vanished through the companionway.

The sky was dirty. A slow wind came in across Tampa Bay, like the hot breath of an eager woman. I started toward the companionway. My foot kicked something that rang on the deck. It was a small brass key, glinting against the mahogany. I reached for it, then pocketed it fast just as Ivor Hendrix came into view again, the white cylindrical purse swinging in her hand.

We made the pier and walked slowly. One of the cops stood looking our way, his arms folded, rocking on his heels. He couldn't make out who we were at this distance.

The girl in the cream-colored suit paused as another cop called to her, moved toward her, talking.

I said, "Easy, now. We've got to make that red outboard. Jump for it. Make it look as normal as possible. I'll unhook the line. Get up in the bow."

She didn't speak. We reached the boat. She jumped, landed rocking wildly. Water splashed over the sides.

"Hey, there!" one of the cops called. He walked slowly toward the pier. The cop talking with the girl, turned, gave a yell and ran toward the sea wall.

"Sit tight," I said.

I snagged the line, whipped it free, and leaped into

the boat. If the motor didn't catch, we were sunk. The sound of that motor would be my excuse later on.

I shoved away from the pier, grabbed the starting rope. I tried to make it all look as ordinary as possible. Very likely it looked like two people trying to escape the police. I whipped the starting rope. The motor coughed twice.

"Hey!" a cop called.

The motor caught, roared violently. I shoved the throttle hard over. The motor blasted into the graying day.

The two cops ran toward the pier. Ivor Hendrix was facing me, clutching the sides with white-knuckled hands, the white purse pinned between her bare knees.

The boat lay on its side as I turned and picked up speed. We walloped the water of the bay, clearing the pier, running close in against the side of the *Carol*. I glanced back. They were running along the pier, waving. One of them had drawn his gun. He wouldn't use it. They would never be certain I'd heard them call.

In no time at all every beach entrance would be watched. They'd have the Coast Guard 'copter out looking for this red outboard.

I felt trapped now. I had to come up with something, and fast. Otherwise, they would eventually find me, and whatever plans I'd had for this town would go up the flue like thin black soot. My chance to locate Hendrix was gone. Whoever was coming for Ivor could have led me to her husband. I'd been unable to take that route.

She sat there watching me, clutching the sides of the boat, her hair gusting in snarls around her pale face, her skirt twisted up across the smooth white thighs.

We approached a narrow finger of land. I cut in around that. Through trees, I saw a road. A police cruiser tore along the road, siren wailing, headed toward Maximo Point. I cut in close to shore. The car vanished. The motor was still wide open.

Out here we were vulnerable. We raced violently past fishing piers now. Suddenly the shoreline changed to jungle. I saw the opening of a mangrove-clotted bayou. I swung in there.

Choppy water changed to grass, and we vaulted snags and roared under a bridge. I slowed the motor, staying well in to shore. Another cruiser flashed across the bayou bridge.

We were on the south side of town. The shoreline changed, and I saw homes set back among trees; the jungle landscape turned to cared-for lawn.

I veered the boat toward a vacant lot, ran it aground. Ivor Hendrix cried out, flipped backward, and sprawled off the seat. Her long legs flashed awry. She righted herself, and we leaped over the side together, landing on silty ground. Fiddler crabs scrambled in rustling waves for their burrowlike homes.

It had been a long time since I'd lived in this town. I remembered this area as pure jungle. It had changed. I didn't know exactly where we were. We ran up across somebody's front lawn and reached a pink cement road.

"We'll have to find a phone," I said.

She breathed heavily, her face sheened with perspiration. The auburn hair was darker at the temples, thickly snarled. I knew people along the bayou would report the red outboard, because the police would probably be airing this on TV.

I said, "We'll use a phone in somebody's home. I'll get a cab and take you someplace. Another motel — that'll give me a little time, anyhow."

We approached a long low white house with a Volkswagon sitting in the gravel drive. I thought of stealing the car. It wouldn't turn the trick.

I rang the bell on the front porch. Ivor Hendrix did quick things to her hair and brushed with finicky strokes at dirt on her skirt.

I experienced a brief moment of dark futility, like being shot at from point-blank range. Then I was all right.

A middle-aged man carrying a newspaper, wearing khaki walking shorts, horn-rimmed glasses, and smoking a pipe, answered the door.

"Could we use your phone?" I said. "Car broke down. I was going to walk to a garage, but there doesn't seem...."

"No garage around here," he said. "Sure. Come in."

We went inside. Ivor Hendrix was as nervous as a cat. She bumped into the corner of a table, gasped, and the man looked at her. He showed me the phone and stood there, banging the newspaper against his leg, blowing smoke.

I called a cab. They said they would be right out. We started for the door. Her eyes were like broken glass.

"Why don't you wait here?"

"Thanks. We'll wait outside."

We went out and crossed the drive and moved down to the curb. We stood under the fragrant shade of a camphor tree, and she leaned back against the trunk, avoiding my eyes, gripping the white purse with both hands, her teeth nibbling her lower lip.

"I keep thinking of Vince," she said. "I can't seem to forget how he looked, lying there. I keep thinking everything's my fault. I can't get it out of my head. I tried to be a good wife to Carl — it didn't work. What could have happened to him? What's he trying to do? Where is he?"

"Money changes people," I said. "Four hundred thousand dollars is a lot of money. That's what's behind all this. The rest doesn't matter. Everything else was just a kind of fuse. It's curious, though, how things happen to people who are ripe for it."

Her eyes widened. "How do you mean that?"

I shrugged. "Everybody I've run into on this thing has been sitting on a keg of emotional dynamite."

"Me, too?"

"You, too. Everybody has his own little world. What he forgets is that sometimes his world has windows. Others like to look in and watch."

"You think the Laketown robbery really has something to do with this?"

"I know it," I said. "The trouble is, that's about all I do know. Vince Gamba was trying to tell me he thought he knew where money was buried. What money? The four hundred thousand dollars? All I can figure is, whoever had it doesn't have it any more. Somebody else has it, and maybe has buried it. But why would they kill him — unless it was so he wouldn't talk. Maybe he talked first. Maybe the money isn't buried any more. Maybe it was never buried. Who knows?"

"You're going to find out, though, aren't you?"

"I've got to find out." I looked at her. "It's my neck if I don't. It could be your neck, too."

"You're doing an awful lot for me."

"For myself, too."

"Yes, but for me."

I reached over and took her hand. "I like doing it for you," I said. "Okay?"

"Okay."

A cab turned the corner down the street and lightly beeped its horn.

From a distance, roofing the cloud-darkening forenoon, the keening sound of a siren reached us.

Her fingers tightened on my hand. "Lee?"

"Yeah?"

"This is the first time I've ever felt secure, protected. It's you, Lee. You're such a wonderful guy."

"I wish to hell you hadn't said that."

"It's how I feel."

"It's going to be damned hard to live up to."

"I mean it."

For a minute, there, I thought the sun was shining. Then the cabby called to us. "You coming, or ain't you coming?"

TWENTY

I took Ivor Hendrix to a hotel called Vista Groves. It was a murky leftover of the twenties, hanging by dirty fingernails and threadbare carpets to the tarnished glitter of a vanished past. The four once-white clapboard stories hunched ghostlike in one of the more elderly residential districts. It was still inhabited by what remained of a few aged pioneering citizens with faces like yesterday's paper dolls, limber only in their memories.

"This room gives me the creeps," she said, looking around at the chairs with dusty antimacassars, the old spool bed, the gold-filigreed gingerbread-heavy dressing table with a mirror so clotted with bygone images it was too tired to reflect today. The room's single bow to modernity was a clashing overhead light fixture. It was a large opaque white glass globe that looked somehow obscene against the cracked, yellow plaster of the ceiling. Around the edges of the ceiling were frescoed flowers. The flowers wept moisture down the high walls in places, like the sparse, crystal tears of the dying.

"You won't be here forever," I said. "And nobody'll find you. That clerk downstairs doesn't even know what year it is."

She sat tentatively on the edge of the bed. We had stopped at Woolworth's and bought two cheap cardboard suitcases. I'd told the clerk she was my sister and that she had come to Florida for an indefinite stay. He was charmed. She had registered as Helen Spencer. It looked legitimate.

"What does 'vine tree' mean?" I said, standing by the door. "I heard you say it over the phone to Elk."

Her face was blank. She shook her head slowly. "You must've misunderstood something." She frowned. "I can't imagine what it could have been. I didn't say anything like that, I'm sure."

"You feel any better? As frightened as you were?"

"You make me feel secure."

We watched each other. I looked her over quietly, and her cheeks picked up some dusty pink. She lifted the edge of the dusty bedspread nervously, to be doing something, and looked at the sheet. She dropped the spread into place and looked up at me again. The eyes were very dark blue, almost black, and they looked hot. The shape of her mouth was suddenly soft and red. Her breasts moved richly with the way she breathed. The dress she wore was filled like a sunshot plum, and my throat thickened, watching her.

She could be a lot more than her sister. We both knew what we were both thinking.

"What's the matter?" she said, knowing very well what was the matter.

I rubbed my hand across my face. "Nothing."

"I'm sorry I got you into this. The police don't like you now, do they?"

I didn't speak.

"What will they do to you?"

"Christ knows," I said. "I've played it all wrong. Instead of working with them, I've worked against them, and now I'm up to my ears."

"Can't you go to them and straighten it out?"

"It would leave me a lot worse off than I am."

"I'd think they would understand if you explained."

"Yeah. It's a good clean way to think."

"It seems awfully long since yesterday afternoon."

"Doesn't it?"

Her eyes lidded self-consciously. "What are you planning?"

I went to the door and took hold of the doorknob, hard. "Not what you think," I said.

"I don't know what you mean."

I looked back at her. She was staring at me wide-eyed. She half smiled. "I wish you'd explain that."

"I'd like to hear myself, too."

"Well?"

"Well, what?"

She brushed at the edge of her skirt on her knee with the backs of her fingers. "I don't like staying here all alone. I'm frightened — something inside me keeps telling me something's going to happen. Couldn't you stay with me a while?" She looked at me crisply.

"That the only reason you want me to stay? Because you're frightened?"

"I don't think so."

I opened the door.

"I think you're terrific," she said. "You're a little crazy, too. Did you know that?"

"Somebody tells me that at least once every day."

"I still think you're terrific."

I opened the door a little more, not feeling at all terrific. I felt lousy, even letting her say that. She didn't know what a bastard I was. "I want you to stay right here," I told her. "Don't go any place. Sit here and wait."

"Okay. You know something? You're very tall and straight. It reminds me of the books I used to read about the pioneers and Indian hunters. Tall and straight as an arrow."

"I'm happy not to return the compliment, if that's what it was, and it shouldn't be. I'll be back for you soon."

"You'd better," she said. "Know what I mean?"

"I'll take a wild guess and say yeah."

"Will you get a shave before you come back?"

"Do I need a shave?"

"Yes."

"Indian hunters never shaved. You want me to get a shave?"

"No."

This could go on all night. I went out into the hall and closed the door. I closed it gently. Then I walked down the hall. I didn't see or recall a single thing until I stood outside on the sidewalk.

Asa and Ivor. A pair of sisters if ever a pair was.

TWENTY-ONE

My head began to pain worse than yesterday. I started walking for the nearest U-Rent-It car emporium. A thin sticky mist fell from the dark blanket of sky. Everybody on the street had suddenly become an informer to the police. They all knew I was trying to hide. The sound of a radio or TV was a siren.

I was a mess.

I dodged into a stand-up lunch counter, ordered coffee and a hamburger that should have been used as a tire on a foreign sports car, and swallowed four more of the yellow tablets the drugstore pharmacist had sold me for my head. Nothing seemed to happen.

There was a round mirror behind the coffee urn. I got a look at myself. I looked as if I'd been shot out of a cannon and the powder charge was a bit heavy.

My eyes were like fifty-caliber bullet holes in a cypress plank. I had been wearing a tie. The knot was swiveled up under my collar wing. The collar itself looked as if some patient ghoul had rubbed tobacco juice into it over a period of days. I started combing my hair with my fingers, struck a tender spot and nearly collapsed with the pain.

Leaning against the counter, I clawed two more of the yellow tablets from the bottle, and fondly gulped them with the last of the coffee. I lit a cigarette, took two drags, and suddenly couldn't see anything. Everything was totally dark. My ears rang. I was stone blind.

I held to the counter, tried not to panic.

In the midst of this I knew what had become of the body. There was no thought to it. It simply struck me, and there it was. Don't tell me the subconscious can't carry its share of the load.

"Something wrong?" somebody asked.

"No," I said. "Just thinking. I'm fine."

They didn't speak again. I would never know who it was. I wouldn't care a hell of a lot, either.

Vince Gamba had found the body. He had been in

love with Ivor, worried about her being mixed up in something bad, and taken the body someplace. It had to be that.

I stood there. The world was an underground midnight. I had to move. I couldn't move. I tried to be nonchalant about the whole thing.

I had no head again. I couldn't see, but of course you have to pay for small considerations. There was no pain anywhere in me. I was as light as a feather, with a sense of well-being like these guys lying in an alley propelled to the other side of paradise on canned heat.

"You better call the hospital," somebody whispered. A corner of light winked in my left eye. A shade began to go up. I began walking blearily, as fast as I could.

"Sir?" somebody called. "Sir?"

I kept walking, out into the street, down in the general direction of the U-Rent-It place. As I walked, my sight cleared and I could see again. Maybe not as well as formerly, but then, what can you expect?

I laughed sharply, took out the bottle of yellow tablets and shot the bottle high out over Central Avenue. I heard it bong off the top of a car, then smash on pavement. I felt better.

I had a pale chance. Anemic, in fact. If either the police, or watermelon-head got to me first, I was cooked crisp. It was probably watermelon-head who had called Ivor on the *Carol*. Only how had he known she was there?

Elk Crafford? I didn't think so. I could be wrong.

Two cops conversed on the corner of Seventh and Central. Another directed traffic a block down. Still another scooted along the curb on a white kiddy-car, with a long chalk-stick, marking cars' tires.

I reached the U-Rent-It place, bought myself a day's worth of Ford sedan, color blue, and hit the road.

The pink Cadillac was parked in front of the Crafford residence. I pulled into the drive behind it and got out. The front glass door swung open. The man who'd been seated on the steps last night stood on the porch, frowning at me.

"Mr. Crafford?"

He nodded. He was bigger than I recalled, standing, with shoulders like a bear under the white jacket that looked as if it had been slept in. His shirt collar was unbuttoned. He had on a wrinkled pair of light blue trousers. His dark hair was longish and sparse, pink skull showing through. His face was meaty and mottled, the eyes sunken, harried, the mouth a broad straight line across the face like a knife gash that wouldn't bleed. It was a mouth that would reveal very little of what went on inside the man.

I told him who I was.

"I've heard about you," he said. He had been drinking, but not enough to count. He had the look of a lush.

He was going to ignore the fact that we'd more or less met last night. He brought out a curved-stem black pipe and stuck it in his mouth, chewing the stem.

"How well do you know your wife's sister?" I said.

"If you expect to shoot questions at me, you may as well quit, right now." He lifted the eyebrows tiredly, and lowered them as if they were too heavy for words.

"If you get me," he added.

"Wanted to ask a favor of you. If you'd answer the one question."

"I know her well enough."

"May as well tell you," I said. "I know you kept her on your schooner last night — that you tried to help her. I've just left her."

He reached up and took the pipe from his mouth. He frowned with that same tired expression, moved down two steps, and stood there looking at me. He turned and glanced back at the house door, then at me again.

"She all right?"

"You think a lot of her."

"Maybe."

"She's okay."

He said nothing.

"Don't you want to know where she is?"

He gave with the eyebrow lift again. Now it was as if he tried to hold himself up with the eyebrows. "What use asking?" he said. "You choose to tell me, you will."

"Are you in love with her?" I watched him closely.

He stared at me, put the pipe in his mouth again, and sat down on the steps, and stared at his hands. He did not speak.

I looked at him, debating. I had to trust someone. Her safety was important in a way beyond these offenses of murder and robbery, in a way I didn't quite understand as yet. It was a selfish and personal importance. At the same time, if her husband or some confederate did discover her, that importance might be nullified. There was no doubt in my mind as to the desperation *somebody* was experiencing at this moment. Your hundred thousand dollars had slipped through somebody's fingers, and they were more than troubled.

I had the strange feeling of being close to some sort of revelation.

Maybe an opiate dream induced by the yellow H-bombs.

I said, "You've accepted the way I've been probing around pretty decently. It's not always that way."

He moved his fingers in a gesture of unconcern.

"I'm on a strange kind of case," I said.

"I know about it," he said. "I wish I could help you. It doesn't seem as if I'm even suspect. I sort of wish I were. I seem to be standing in the middle of everything. It's the story of my life. I'm involved in everything, yet I'm only a bystander. It has a strange twist of humor, if you regard it from the proper angle."

"I imagine so," I said. "You have any stray thoughts? Bystanders sometimes see things."

He looked at me. "I'm loaded with stray thoughts," he said. "Stray thoughts and alcohol. That's about the extent of it, I'm afraid. You're in a jam, aren't you? I mean, with the city police — the sheriff's department. It's a crazy sort of thing, isn't it? I mean, you can't ring up the usual case against possible suspects, because motivations don't necessarily jibe."

"There's always motivation for murder," I said.

"Well, I don't know of anyone who's messed up in this who wouldn't have reason to kill somebody else concerned. Me included," he said. "And not alone for that money." He rolled up eyes upward. "That is one hell of a lot of money."

"Isn't it?"

He looked at me and shook his head. "It's all on television," he said. "The whole business. You, the police, the bodies, the bank robbery. The works. Christ, they're troubled about you. Really, you know? I don't see how you stand a chance. How the hell you've eluded them so far is beyond me. They're after you, chum."

"You could turn me in."

"I'm a bystander, remember?" He coughed lightly. "I don't turn people in."

I said, "Listen, I'm going to tell you something, that's why I'm here." I told him where she was and asked him to keep it to himself. He didn't say anything. "I wanted to tell somebody. She's registered under the name Helen Spencer."

"Thanks for the trust. You probably shouldn't have told anyone. Since it's me, you haven't any worries. I guess Carl flipped his stupid lid."

"Did Ivor tell you about this Vince Gamba?"

He nodded. "Pretty broken up about that."

I said, "Somebody called her at the *Carol*. They threatened her. They said they were calling for Carl. How would anyone know she was there?"

"You've got me. I didn't tell anyone."

"You don't seem concerned."

"I'm a — "

"You're a bystander, remember — yeah." I began to wish I hadn't told him. "You're not a bystander where she's concerned. Don't kid me."

"Yes, I am. Whether I like it or not."

I looked up and saw Asa Crafford coming down the inside hall, walking fast. She must have heard our voices.

"I'm moving on," I said.

He'd caught the movement of my eye. "Yeah. Good luck."

I walked over to the car. As I backed out of the drive, Asa Crafford flourished onto the porch. Elk turned and stared at her, then down at his hands again. She watched me get the Ford in motion as I went down the street.

It had begun to rain. It was the same vertical mist of yesterday. The streets were mirrored and slippery.

My windshield shattered. Something smacked into the back of the seat beside my shoulder. Dust puffed. The car slid out of control for a moment.

It took me a full three seconds before I realized I'd been shot at.

Then I saw the maroon Olds.

TWENTY-TWO

I stood on the loud pedal.

The Olds roared at me from a side street curb where it had been parked. He'd probably been waiting for me to appear at the Crafford house. I couldn't see the driver's face behind the wheel. He had the engine wide open.

The Ford began to wind up. I had no gun. I was sure the driver of the other car was the imported heavy who had bolixed up my skull. He had a .45 automatic that I knew of. There was no telling what extra artillery he carried.

A dirt street joined the street I was on. The intersection was a mass of pot-holes. I took the turn in a wallow of mud and bottoming springs. I braked, turned at the next right, opened the engine wide again. It was a hump-backed asphalt road, gleaming like ice in the misting rain. The Ford seemed to hit lightly along the surface, the wheel like a thin piece of wire in my hands. The tires sizzled like bacon frying.

The windshield was fouled with dust and rain. It formed an opaque mass in front of my eyes. The wipers refused to operate, or I didn't know how to work the switch. I glanced in the rear-view mirror. The Olds was perceptibly gaining. The droning whine of the powerful engine creased the roar of the Ford.

A broad stretch of brick pavement veered diagonally off to the right into what I knew was a sedate residential section, constructed along the old nineteen-twenty boom-period scheme of roads. The landscape was jungle. Trees dropped low over the bricks. The streets in here were a jumble of hairpin turns, small circles — a labyrinthian maze.

I headed in there. The Olds, following, slid viciously across the brick, straightened. I knew I had to get away from that car, that man, or die. There was no other answer.

The guy was out to get me one way or another. There would be no more bargaining now.

I drove through an unhoused area, starting around a broad circle. The circle of ground was covered only with grass and a few large water oaks.

He began firing at me again.

I was a good target. There was nothing I could do. We were at opposite sides of the circle, which composed an area slightly larger than an average city block. There were no streets leading off the circle. I hunched down as far as I could, then realized that if he hit the metal of the door with one of those slugs, it would tear through into me as if it weren't even there.

I glanced over toward him. Two slugs ripped through the car to the rear of the front seat. At the same instant, he savagely turned the Olds up over the curbing. He came powering directly at me across the stretch of browned grass between the trees.

Another car approached me from the opposite direction. I passed it and met the street where I had turned onto the circle. It was then I realized I was lost in here.

At one time I'd known this crazy-house of streets. No more. If I didn't get out of here, I might inadvertently trap myself on a dead-end.

To top it off, the windshield was nearly blind. I worked nervously with the wiper switch. Nothing happened. It wasn't raining hard enough to erase the contamination of slime on the glass. I put my head out the side window, trying to see ahead. It wasn't much better. I couldn't control the car well at speed.

I hit a straight flat street and pressed the accelerator down again. He was back there, sliding in a shriek of rubber on a turn. The Olds straightened and flew at me as if shot out of a gun. I was finished unless I pulled a trick out of the hat.

I wondered if any of the old wooded section down by

the bay was left.

I swerved right, the left wheels up over the curb, lurching through a long, slow curve. The pavement bricks were so slick I couldn't get back on the street. The car was on the edge of going completely out of control. I knew if I touched the brakes I was done. I held it, and gradually crept back toward the street, the wheels lurched and sang across bricks. Some of these streets were deadends. If I happened to be on one of them, he would have me.

The road ceased. Curbs beveled into the rutted grass. I drove straight on through the opening where the street had been planned, no chance for hesitation, trusting to the memory of possible lovers' lanes. This had always been necking country in the old days, and it didn't look much changed. The wheels struck a battering bump. The windshield wipers began working, smearing at the murky mess on the glass, helping a little bit.

I drove through woods, turning toward the bayside. As a rule, car paths led out from parking areas on the bay in all directions. I kept it wide open. White-blue waters of the bay flashed between trees.

A car parked up ahead suddenly leaped into gear, slid in a tire-biting turn, and shot toward me, rocking. A guy and his gal. As we passed, I saw her face, the gaping red mouth, the wide eyes, as she struggled to pull down her skirt. They'd figured I was copper. The guy hunched low over the wheel, really driving. He didn't look my way.

I watched the rear-view mirror as much as I dared. I saw the Olds slamming between trees. The two cars approached each other. The guy and his gal were going like hell now. The Olds broke and pulled off the lane among thicker trees, avoiding collision.

I bounced lurching into a beaten clearing beside the bay, saw another cut-off leading through thickly growing vines. I took it, the tires grinding through deep ruts.

In another instant I burst out on brick pavement, sliding sidewards. I straightened out against the far curb, took the next left, and a half minute later came out on smooth asphalt. It was Twenty-Second Avenue, which would lead me straight to Forty-Ninth, and on to Pine Park.

There was no sign of the Olds. I'd lost him.

The Ford made like a baby jet. We went.

I crossed through most of town without trouble. Still on Forty-Ninth. I began to relax, and then I saw the police cruiser. It rolled slowly toward me. They were taking their time, looking. They could have checked the U-Rent-It spots. It could well be that they knew what I was driving because I'd had to give my right name when I rented the Ford.

I turned fast into an alley, cut the engine beside an old red cement house, and lay low on the seat.

Cracking the door, I looked out. They slowly drove past. I waited. They were gone. I stuck my head up and saw the cruiser parked directly across the street opposite the mouth of the alley. White smoke powdered from the exhaust. They had me.

I started out of the car, casing the alley for a run. Then I saw they had stopped for the corner red light.

Two cops sat in the cruiser, batting the breeze. I

climbed back under the wheel. If they turned their heads, they would see me. They would be checking every blue Ford sedan in the city.

They drove off.

I sat there. My shirt stuck to my back with perspiration. My palms were slick on the wheel rim. There was a fine trembling all through me. I was getting old and crochety and all used up. I felt lousy.

I drove on toward Pine Park. The overalled, tobacco-spitting fat man with the crowbar was still there beside the road, probing in his drainage ditch. He waved. Maybe he would always be there.

I parked in the same spot as yesterday, overlooking the lake and the trailer, and walked down toward the cement block house.

It was still. Wind breathed in treetops, and the mist had thinned. More and more I sensed the spot I was on. They would be looking for me everywhere. There was no safe place to be.

The door of the cement block house was open.

I jammed my hands in my pockets, scowled at the whole rotten business. I stood there staring at the shackles and chains. My hand touched something in my pocket. I felt as if somebody had stuck a hatpin into the back of my neck. I saw myself going to Elk Crafford, telling him where Ivor Hendrix was.

I was the worst kind of fool. It was a wonder I was able to remember my name.

I took the brass key out of my pocket. I had found it on the deck of Crafford's schooner, the *Carol*. If it happened to fit the padlock on those chains, I had possibly thrown her to the dogs. I had completely forgotten about the key. Of course, it wouldn't fit.

I grabbed up the padlock, the chains rattling. The brass key slid into the slot like you'd stick your finger in butter, and it turned those tumblers quicker than Florene could turn a trick at the old Parsienne Sphinx. Florene had been fast. She was a piker compared to this key. I stood up, holding the key, thinking how crazy the comparison was. I felt crazy. You have to be crazy to be as stupid as I'd been.

I turned and ran for the car.

Savage noises reached from up on the knoll beyond the lake. They were animalistic, nightmarish. I ran on past the trailer. The trash pit where they had burned things was cleaned out. There was no sign of the suitcase. I moved fast up past the lake through wet knee-high brown grass. Reaching the slope of the knoll, I entered thick pine woods. The sounds coming from in there would make violent death an anemic dream.

I stopped. My insides lifted sickeningly.

It was the hound. Out of sight, out of mind. Vince Gamba's dog. Snarling, it gripped a human hand in its teeth. It yanked ferociously at an arm, tearing it from a freshly scarred hole gouged in the soft earth.

The animal's eyes were a red frenzy. White fangs sank deep into the stiff claw of hand. The dog's body was braced as it yanked and viciously whipped its head. The arm came free. The beast growled in its throat, lashed its head. The arm flew off into the grass. The hound dove into the pit, its blood singing with ancestral cravings on distant moonlit plains. The teeth ripped into a man's ankle, bare and paper-white above a dirty tennis shoe.

I yelled at the hound, ran at him, trying to scare him off.

It whirled, stood braced, head down, eyes up, jaws open, and emitted a crazed whine.

I ran at it again. It stood ground.

The hound had dug the earth free revealing the muddy corpse of the man I'd found shackled in the cement block house. The body lay in a crumpled, awkward position, smeared with wet dirt.

We faced each other across the corpse.

"Go home, boy!"

It was then I saw the scar; a raised, bloody, festering welt on the dead man's abdomen.

This was Barton Yonkers. Somebody had killed him for four hundred thousand grand. That same somebody could put me right beside him. Everything had turned into a crumbling house of paper cards.

The hound did not move. I ran at it again, shouting. It stood ground, the wild light in its eyes unchanged.

I turned, looking around in the grass for a length of limb, something to go after the hound with.

I continued to stand in a twisted position, staring.

Steifer and Vagas walked toward me. They were about fifteen feet away. Steifer held a gun in his hand.

"Stand still," he said.

I straightened slowly. I felt something go out of me, like life, maybe, or hope. Something else took it place. It was a kind of raw and violent despair.

TWENTY-THREE

Rudy Vagas wore a yellow oilsilk slicker. His eyes grinned, but the rest of his face was a dead thing to see. Steifer had on a black raincoat. The two of them moved closer. They looked at the body in the muddy grave. They looked at the mute hound. Then they looked at me.

Steifer wagged his gun and wiped his face with his free hand.

"We've been trying to locate you," he said.

"I've been kind of busy."

They stared at the body.

"This dog found it," I said. "Nasty, isn't it?"

"I'd say it was crazy," Vagas said. "Must we stand around here?"

The hound made no sound. It seemed to be waiting now, interest in the corpse gone. I only had half listened to what Vagas said. I knew I had to get back to the Vista Groves Hotel, where Ivor Hendrix waited. I felt the tight drawstrings of desperation. I couldn't breathe right. I felt blocked.

"Must have been a surprise," Steifer said. His voice was like the taste of alum. "Having that little old hound-dog dig up the body like this."

"What are you getting at?"

"We have a warrant for your arrest, Baron," Vagas said. "Don't make things worse for yourself, and worse for us."

"What conditions?"

"Material witness. Withholding evidence. Aiding and abetting. Conspiring with criminals. Breaking and entering. Disturbing the scene of a crime. You name it." He let his eyes go narrow. "Suspicion of homicide."

My throat was dry. When I spoke, my voice cracked.

"You know better than that."

"Do we?"

"I just came out here in line with...."

"So did we. When the medical examiner gets here, along with Sheriff Silverman, and Haddock — and the lab crew, the newspaper crew — we'll have a real party."

I didn't say anything.

Steifer said, "Some kid coming home from school, playing hooky, heard the dog. He came over to investigate. He saw what was going on, ran home, and his mother called the sheriff's department. Silverman and Haddock are working together on this. Silverman's coming with a couple deputies, they ought to be here. We're tired. Can you imagine that?"

"No kid saw me," I said. "I just got here."

"We didn't figure you sat up with that," he said, gesturing toward the body. There was real irritation in his tone now. His voice lowered. "You think we want to believe a guy like you would get himself fouled up in something like this? Give us some credit."

They were closing in. How do you get away from two trained cops. Especially when they're carrying a grudge.

Steifer's voice was bitter. "You bastard," he said. "You know goddamned well we've been trying to locate you. You've been staying out of our way. It's been a game of tag to you, you son-of-a-bitch. So now we've got you. Using a friend, too. Hoagy Stills came to Haddock with the information on that gun right after he talked with you. That was a *great* way to act. With us right there, talking to Stills. You sure as hell are a son-of-a-bitch, Baron — believe me. We got no sympathy for a louse like you." He raised his voice. "Every lawman in the state working day and night. And you playing tiddly-winks with hot information, using it to your own purposes."

"And a tiddly-wink to you," I said.

Vagas thrust his lower lip out. "Where is that money, Baron? That's what you've been after, isn't it? Playing your neat lone game."

My voice was strained through chips of broken glass. "There's no use in my trying to tell you anything. You've got it all figured out. You know all the answers. The oracles of Central Homicide." I spoke evenly. "You're so thick-skulled you wouldn't recognize the truth if it gnawed holes in your head." I looked at the hound. He was trotting around in the grass, panting. I said, "I came out here to see what I could find. It was a logical place to pick up threads. Also, I found a key today — a key that fits the padlock on those chains down there in that cement block house, where that corpse," I turned and pointed, "was when I first found him." I had half an angle. It was the lousy half, as usual, but I decided to play it out and see what happened. Only the instant I'd finished speaking, I felt as if I'd turned a gun on myself. Naturally, to them, I *would* have the key.

"Sure," Steifer said. "It figures. But why tell us you

'found' the key?" He turned to Vagas. "He's crawling, Rudy. Like the worm he is. Trying to crawl out from under."

I spoke to Rudy Vagas. "This body, here, is Barton Yonkers. The same guy who clobbered the Laketown bank. His pal, Horace Ailings, is dead. The body was found over by Lake Wales. Doesn't that mean anything to you?"

Vagas snorted mildly. "Let's see the key, bright boy. Take it easy — toss it to me."

I tossed him the damned key.

"Hold him right here and let him suffer," Vagas said. "I'll be back in a minute." He turned and started off down the slope toward the trailer.

Steifer and I watched each other.

"I know what's in your head," he said. "I'd kill you."

I said, "Your brains wear shoes."

He said, "Where's the money, Baron?"

I looked at the hound. It was as if he were guarding the dead body, now. I was soaking wet with sweat.

Steifer said, "Why don't you level with me? You know you haven't got a chance." He glanced down through the woods, where Vagas had walked. "Come on," he said. "Spill it to me. You've got this Hendrix dame someplace, right? Why not tell it? Tell it to me. You got a heat on for her, only she wants money to play the game. You started out on this thing somehow, and you saw a chance to really make a killing. Isn't that right?"

I said, "You're sure new in those clothes you're wearing. I'll bet you're back in uniform by tomorrow."

He took a quick step toward me, ready to say

something else, troubled.

I said, "Trying to work it so you'll get the gold star while your pal Rudy's not in sight?"

Steifer moved another quick step. It scared the hound briefly. The hound leaped, snarling at him, like a horse shying. Steifer instinctively looked down and lashed out with his right hand, his gun hand. I moved.

I chopped and caught him with a judo clip on the side of the neck. He dropped the gun. I'd had to do it. His eyes were astonished in that spare second before I chopped him again, giving it everything. Halfway down, he tried to call out. I went crazy, fingered my fists into a club, and smashed him on the joint of skull and neck, at the back, with all my strength. He huddled in a ball on his knees and flattened out, cold.

I was already running when I remembered Vagas. The hound stood over Steifer, mouth gaping. I had to get to the Ford. Vagas was in the cement block house now. If I went for the car, I'd be directly in his line of fire.

I ran as softly as I could down the slope toward the trailer. I started around behind it, then remembered the letters from Asa Crafford to Carl Hendrix, behind the veneer in the closet. There might not be another chance to get them. I slipped along the front of the trailer. The door was open. I went in fast, over to the closet. The closet door was open. The veneer was down among the shoes, with the bottle of gin. The letters were gone.

I got out of there fast, went behind the trailer. I walked now, on my heels, digging them into the ground, without sound. I weighed a straight two hundred. I had put all I could of that weight onto Steifer's neck and skull. Again, as with the punk Joe Lager, I hoped to God I hadn't killed him. I never used that method without worrying. One time I'd killed a man that way. The memory of it was bad. He'd been due to die, but Steifer was just the north end of a horse headed south.

I came around the side of the cement block house, listening, and reached the door. Vagas was hunkered down trying the key in the padlock. He hadn't heard me. Then I heard the hound coming, crashing through the grass and brush, like the devil was after him.

Vagas heard him, too.

I didn't wait.

He turned straight into my fist as I lifted it from the floor. It caught his jaw. His teeth cracked. He arched backward, his eyes gone up into his skull. I stood there with my wrist and elbow a blaze of sharp pain, my knuckles numbed. When the feeling returned to my knuckles, it was like being struck with a hammer. I had smashed a knuckle.

Vagas' gun was on the dirt floor. I kicked it into shadows under the army cot. He got to his knees, groaning, then fell back.

"I'm sorry," I said. "But you wouldn't listen. I've got things to do, and you couldn't let me go."

He kept talking Martian, saliva running down his lips, trying to get up. Again he got to his knees and fell back. I grabbed up the length of chain, wrapped it around his leg, and snapped the padlock on it. The key twinkled on the floor. I got that and fired it out the door, then turned, running.

The hound watched balefully. He didn't move as I ran past him, heading for the Ford.

Two long strides past the doorway, slugs ripped into the dirt by my feet, and I heard the shots rattle off across the country. Steifer was up on the knoll. He wasn't sure whether or not I had Vagas's gun.

"Baron!" Steifer shouted. "Don't be a fool!"

I ran like hell for a wooded slope to the left. There was no chance to make the Ford now. I had to reach the shelter of woods. He would shoot to kill.

"Baron — *stop!*"

He fired again. I kept going. He was being careful. A careful cop is a deadly cop. The slug ticked a pine, ricocheted skyward in a snarling whine.

I ran head down, my feet sliding on the ground. I came over the top of the slope, looked back there. Steifer knelt on the opposite knoll, beside Yonkers' grave. He took aim, holding the gun with both hands.

I dropped. The slug cracked over my head.

I rolled across clean wet grass, glimpsing splashes of misty sky, then smelling the sharp wet odor of the earth. I came up running. I was in pine woods.

Steifer's voice echoed.

"Stop — *Baron!*"

I ran with everything I had, tasting gall in my throat, feeling the urgent labor of my lungs. A loud snapping and snarling and crashing was behind me. It was the hound.

He ran jawing beside me. His eyes were full of laughter. For a brief instant both of us rushed back through the years to the time when I was a boy, running through damp autumnal Montana fields with my own dog leaping at my side. Long ago, before the family migrated to Florida, before James Baron had thought of becoming a private cop.

I paused, listening. My breath rasped rawly in my throat. Steifer let go another shot. It was wild. He called, out of range now. Then he began running. He crashed toward me, distantly.

"Home, boy!" I said to the hound.

The hound lolled his tongue, eyes dancing. He was ready for the race. I ran again. The dog kept pace in a lazy lope.

Steifer fired. The slug whipped through trees. I spotted a road, a billboard advertising women's bathing suits. The sound of a siren lifted like an emotional wrench through the quiet day.

I was back where I'd come from. In my mind's eye, I saw them — piling out of police cars, shouting orders, starting through the woods in pursuit.

Lines of blue. Neighbors would be deputized by Sheriff Zack Silverman. All out for the monster.

I leaped a ditch onto a macadam road. I was dragging lead now. I ran off in the direction of town. As I ran, I tried to beat some of the dirt off my clothes, thinking of trying to hail a ride. In ten minutes, this area would swarm with law like bacteria on an infected wound. Men with shotguns. They would have the 'copter out. Field glasses and scopes.

I jogged steadily along.

You read about them, trying to escape the Law. They must know it's only a matter of time. You can't escape the Law. It's organized. You can't escape today's organization. I knew this. There is only the momentary respite. The emotions of this moment, knowing you're wrong, knowing they *will* get you; the feeling of overwhelming doom, of being trapped, knowing you can easily be killed even when fundamentally guiltless — this feeling is comparable to nothing. The doom is complete. Convention reads it to you from the crib; the Law is the force of right — right *or* wrong — and if you err, you pay. There is no escape. In the close chase, you run hand in hand with doom. You don't dismiss panic. Panic is your heart. Panic is your hide. And panic is selfish.

The If — always the If.

If I didn't reach Ivor Hendrix, get her some place else to safety, and locate a tangible fact that would open this case and clear me, I was done. I would rot behind Raiford's bars. It would take more than theory. I had to come up with total answers now.

I couldn't wait for a cab, and a city bus wouldn't serve. The only answer was to steal a car and head for the Vista Groves Hotel.

The hound loped along beside me. I didn't have the strength to order him away. He looked happy, and as crazy as I felt.

I ran past houses, set back off the street now. Then I spotted an Amoco service station on the next corner. Nobody was at the gasoline pumps, no sign of action. A yellow and black '55 Dodge sedan was parked alongside the station. I cut across a vacant lot, approached the station from the rear. The dog prowled beside me. I patted his head, said, "Hush, boy." He looked up at me and laughed sadly.

I reached the car, opened the driver's door, checked

the ignition. Keys hung in the lock. Somebody was talking inside the office. I pushed the shift lever into neutral, released the parking brake, and shouldered the car backward down a gentle cement ramp toward the street. It rolled easily. The hound sat in the middle of the street, head cocked, watching.

The car rolled faster. I got under the wheel, backed into a drive, closed the door, started the engine, and took off in the opposite direction.

There was whining, leaping, scrabbling beside the car. The hound was doing a good forty-five miles an hour, right outside, tongue flapping over his shoulder.

I slammed on the brakes, flung open the door. He leaped in, jumped in back, flinging mud around on the bright parrot-yellow upholstery. He sank down on the seat, meek-eyed, tail flipping. I started off again. Through the rear-view mirror, the gas station back there was quiet.

It began to mist more thickly. A wind came in from the Gulf of Mexico, full of salt, fanning the land. I had a stitch in my side like a rusty knife scraping the muscles of my heart, and I thought of Ivor Hendrix, and of the long ago when we'd known each other, and of the years between — and now.

In every way, Ivor was still more than I could ever have imagined she might have been. You weren't supposed to be able to go back to that first dream — she was only supposed to be a ghost that haunted your lonelier nights.

Something attained, yet never attainable.

Held, yet never again beheld.

Only you had to hope, because without hope, there

was nothing.

I cornered fast at a light and drove across town to the Vista Groves Hotel, hoping.

TWENTY-FOUR

As I walked down the hall toward Ivor Hendrix's room, I suddenly didn't want to look inside the door. It was as if I knew she would be in there, bug-eyed and purple-faced. Or spread across the bed, naked, with a knife sticking in her back.

I rapped lightly. "Ivor?"

She didn't answer.

The door was locked. I backed off, set my heel and let the door have it brutally, just under the lock. The door snapped with shuddering crack, lashed open, back against the inside wall.

You know you're right, you hope you're not right.

It's like getting hit twice as hard the second time, in the same place as the first.

She was gone. Not just dead. Gone.

The room looked as if it had been passed through a threshing machine. It was demolished.

I had done all this by myself.

I closed the door, looked around. Whoever they were, they had gotten to her at last. The place had been picked apart with destructive meticulousness. They had been after something. What?

Elk Crafford's name was a tantalizing whisper. I had told him where she was. If he had harmed her, I would harm him, thoroughly, completely. Ivor Hendrix had gotten to me in her own strangely cool way.

The room was dim, lighted only by a bed lamp. I checked the bathroom. The top was off the water tank on the toilet. The medicine chest had been excavated, the floor littered with smashed bottles, tubes and boxes, leftovers from former tenants.

In the other room, the mattress had been knifed and sliced; stuffing oozed out, bulging among twisted steel springs. Bureau and dressing-table drawers were yanked out, smashed, cleaned. The carpet had been torn up. The shades were ripped from the windows. Curtains had been pulled down.

It had become darker outside. Small rain ticked against the windows. I moved to the wall, switched on the overhead light. It came on brightly. I stared at the big round white globe, stared at a dark elongated shadow.

The high ceiling was faintly stained. Coolness warped along the nape of my neck.

It had been in the movie, *The Lost Weekend*, where Don Birnam hid his whisky up there. Only how would I reach the globe?

How had she reached it? I could be wrong.

I stood on the foot of the bed. Flailing the air with my hand, I was still five feet from the light. The long shape of Ivor Hendrix's cylindrical white purse was quite plain to me now.

I leaped high off the bed, reaching, and missed, thundering to the floor. A brass candlestick lay on the torn carpet, knocked from a shelf. I reached for it, tossed it straight up at the overhead light and ducked.

Glass cracked and showered down. It tinkled and

crashed on the floor. I watched her purse strike the floor and bounce. Something jumped out of the purse, bounding across the room. Whatever it was nestled up against the baseboard by the door.

I listened. There was no sound from the hall.

I went over to the baseboard and picked up the bundle of what looked like small notebooks, held together with a narrow pink garter.

I frowned, stripped the garter off, and shuffled through flat small tan envelopes. I opened one and looked at it, knowing already what they were.

Bank books.

The one I had opened was issued to a woman. Name of Gertrude Paulding. Fort Myers.

It was a new account. I checked the deposit. One thousand, eight hundred.

I looked at another.

Ivor Heira. Lincoln Trust, Hibiscus City, Florida. One thousand, two hundred.

Interested, I opened another bank book. They were very neat, clean, brand-new bank books. They seemed to be all savings accounts. Of course, stupid of me. There was no chance overlooking the interest accumulate.

Henrietta A. Zonders. Key West. Thirty-two thousand.

Another: Loretta Stitskin. West Palm Beach. Fifteen thousand.

Getting a bit bold.

Charlotte Debra Westmark. Miami. Thirty-two thousand.

Babette Jardin. Gainesville. Seventeen thousand.

She got around a lot while she was visiting dear Auntie Liz, up in Orlando. I went over and sat on the ragged mattress, on the bed, and continued with my research. As I opened each bank book, crisply untouched, my heart rocked faintly, and I perspired slightly, and I wanted to throw up.

Mary Fuchs. Jacksonville. Nine thousand.

I hurled that one savagely across the room.

Doubtless playing her little games to while away the wearisome days of travel fatigue.

Alice Botkins Somersall. Tampa. Forty-four thousand.

Grace Golden. Planter's Trust, Orange Corners. Four thousand.

Aileen Fielding Singer. Probably a sewing machine store across the street, there in Bradenton. Twenty-three thousand.

Helene Demmonds Dartell. Miami. Fifty-six thousand.

"I'm so sorry I forgot to tell you, Lee. We can phone Aunt Liz right now, while I'm here. She'll verify that I asked her not to tell anyone I was there."

They call it *brass*.

Barbara Penny. Fort Lauderdale. Thirty-three thousand.

Virginia Allsworth Kring. Boca Raton. Twenty-one thousand.

Vicki Amont. Miami. Thirteen thousand. Each time she was in Miami, she became faintly continental, *chic, or* downright supercilious in her choice of names.

Ruth Mary Allswell. Damned confident. St. Petersburg. Forty-three thousand.

Mimi Loveall. Venice. One thousand, two hundred.

Betty Smythe. De Land. Six thousand.

Marie Fitz-Simmons. Sarasota. Thirty-six thousand.

Margaret Dee Switz. She had glanced at her watch. Pahokee. Twelve thousand.

Nineteen different banks. Over four hundred thousand dollars. All of Florida searching desperately for that money. All of Florida well covered with it.

I stood up, retrieved the bank book I'd hurled across the room. I bundled them neatly together again, snapped the snappy pink garter around them, and dropped them into my pocket — or rather, stuffed them.

I checked her purse. I found a small silver bottle opener from the Mingo Club, in the shape of a dancing girl. Three pencil stubs, well worn with figuring the take, probably. Two lipsticks. A broken jade comb. A broken mirror. Two knotted handkerchiefs, one with three pennies tied in it. Some scraps of paper. A bent cigarette covered with her lipstick. A swizzle stick from some joint called The Silver Lagoon. A ribbon, a hank of hair....

I quit. I dropped the purse and got out of there.

I wasn't sick. I was crazy.

TWENTY-FIVE

In the car, I looked at the hound. He opened one eye, yakked softly, wagged his tail, gaped with a crack, miffed and maffed, then closed the eye and went to sleep again. He snored faintly.

I thought back on things she had told me. The things ticked off in my mind like the fond sound of breaking pretzel sticks. Sometimes that's how it is, when it's raining outside, and growing dark, and you're carrying nineteen bank books in your pocket.

I knew what I'd been doing all this for. Getting myself fouled up and ready for the royal screwing. The one with the luscious auburn hair and the sad, winning smile, and the troublesome skirts, and the faintly-slanted dark blue eyes that could look at you and make you lose sleep.

That's who I'd been doing it for.

My jaws ached with keeping my teeth clamped together so I wouldn't yell.

I started the engine and drove across town without seeing a single cop.

I saw her in my mind's eye. Running around Florida, popping into banks to start just one more savings account.

Planning for the future.

The pink Cadillac was nowhere to be seen at the Canawlside Drive address. I told the hound to stick where he was and ran across the lawn to the front porch.

The door chimes chimed delicately. A drape had been drawn across the entrance glass panels.

I left the porch after a moment, went around the side of the house, through dipping oleanders, jumping azealea bushes. I passed a clump of punk trees and stepped onto a broad patio. Half of it was enclosed by a screen. An archway led into the house. It was open.

More glass doors.

Inside, I moved fast through the house. Nobody in the living room. Somebody had been doing some heavy drinking at the bar. Several bottles stood on the bar, opened; brandy and gin, mostly. Melting ice cubes were scattered across the thick carpet. The cubes weren't far gone, indicating someone had been here shortly before.

I went upstairs. The rooms were debatable reading material, but deserted of human life.

Door chimes rang. Inside the house, the sound of the chimes was dreamy. They rang everywhere, musical and sweet. The sound made me angrier than I was. I tried not to let it.

As I reached the head of the stairs, the chimes ceased. I ran fast along the broad landing on deep carpeting. At a large amber glass window in an arched alcove at the front of the house, I stopped, looked out.

It was the big guy, watermelon-puss; the same handler of skull-crushing .45's I'd had dealings with. Seeing him made my cracked knuckle ache. He was moving down across the lawn toward the curb.

The yellow Dodge sedan I'd swiped was parked down past the boundary of the Crafford lot. He didn't give it a second glance. I saw nothing of the maroon Olds.

The guy opened the door and slid under the wheel of a light gray forty-nine two-door Ford sedan. For a moment I felt cool, then remembered Ivor Hendrix telling me about a similar car. I recalled something else and looked at the right front wheel of the Ford. The hubcap was missing.

I ran hard for the stairs, took them close to headlong,

and struck the marble hall sliding. I ran for the front doorway. I got the first of the big glass doors swung open in time to see outside through a crack in the drawn drapes. The Ford pulled speeding away from the curb.

Outside, I made the Dodge, got it underway. I trailed in the direction the Ford had gone. It was no dice. He had flown. I drove around the nearby blocks, but saw nothing.

It was helplessness I felt now. The anger was turned against myself, precipitating bitterness and despair. It was as if the gods had strained all the fine, subtle futilities of the world through their suddenly partial sieve and packaged them for me, covered with godly gall, the very bitterest of all.

Then I thought of the dead. The late dead of my own concern — Yonkers, Ailings — and Vince Gamba. And they, too, were turned on the spit of futility, skull-grinning midst the ferocity of vanquished desires.

So she could have reasons too. Not just because it was four hundred thousand dollars. You could try to understand that, or you could let it go.

There was little left that wasn't obvious to me, now. The one thing I couldn't understand was how to dig myself free of this mess.

Because I could taste the earth against my teeth.

I drove toward Calcutta Shores.

The Yacht Club was deserted in the rain. The striped umbrellas on the lawn were folded down like the self-consciously lidded eyes of a whore's mother who'd met a priest in the street. Beyond the gently streaming windows of the clubhouse I heard the melancholy tink and boop of ginned-up piano.

I walked along the pier until I reached the *Carol*.

"Knew you'd get here."

Elk Crafford stood up there on the bow against the dark pall of sky over Tampa Bay. He held a bottle in one hand and a shotgun in the other. His eyes were menacing.

"You come up here," he said.

He still wore the white dinner jacket, but with no shirt now, and a pair of red-striped pajama pants. He looked as if he'd been used as a sea-anchor on the Queen Elizabeth.

"You don't need that gun," I said.

"Hurry up," he said.

I walked up the gangplank. He was very drunk.

"Say I don't need this gun?" he said. "Don't I, really? You trying to tell me I don't need this gun?"

I stood four feet from him on the deck.

I said, "Yes. That's right."

His mouth sagged, slaver running from one corner. He cradled the gun in his left arm. His finger was on the trigger. It was an automatic. He dangled the bottle from his other hand by the neck, like a slain animal. Gravity on the bottle threatened to tip him over. He was a thoroughly practiced drunk, probably carrying six times the amount of alcohol an average man could stand up with.

"Oh, hell," he said. He turned away. He took the shotgun in a backswing and hurled it straight up and out over the cabin of the *Carol*. I heard it splash in the bay.

My voice was distant. "Where's Ivor Hendrix?"

He looked at me with hair falling in his eyes. "How hell do I know?"

I felt if I touched him I would kill him.

I shouted at him. "Where is she!"

He stared.

"You son-of-a-bitch," I said. "I told you where she was. She's gone. You're the only one who knew. I found the key to the padlock right on the deck where you're standing."

His head moved slowly back and forth. If he was acting, he deserved a stage. There was a sharp pain in my stomach; the old ulcer starting in again. I tried hard not to step in and hit him.

"Where's your wife?" I heard myself say.

He pitched his head back and roared with angry laughter. His face got red. The veins choked with blood. The eyes bugged redly, like bleeding thumbs. He staggered violently backward, brought himself up sharply against the cabin. Something fell and broke inside.

"Thought I would fall, didn't you?"

His articulation was good.

"I don't care if you fall overboard and drown. Not at all."

"Yes," he said. "That's the right answer to that. Anybody would give me that answer."

He drank moistly from the bottle. Some of it ran down his chin. He let his arm droop again. Whisky sloshed onto the deck.

"What key?" he said. "What padlock?"

"Where did your wife go?"

"You want a lay? That it?"

I said nothing.

He dropped his chin on his chest, watching me all the while.

"She's not here," he said.

"Not home, either."

"Went downtown. Crazy wild insane bitch. I love her." He looked at me. Tears sprang to his eyes. "I love her, you hear?" He wiped the tears with the back of the hand holding the bottle. Whisky spilled. "Crazy, isn't it?"

"It's understandable."

He groaned quietly. "Don't feed me any of that goddam crap."

"She went downtown?"

He nodded, pointed, dropped the bottle. It smashed. Whisky streamed around the deck, reeking pungently. He stared at the puddle.

"Doesn't matter," he said. "Got eight cases aboard. Matter at all."

"Why do you have the gun?" I said. "Who were you expecting?"

"Christ," he said. "I worked myself up to it. I thought I would have it out with him."

He turned and fumbled along the cabin to the companionway, and fell through the hatch. He didn't touch a step. He landed thickly. I looked down. He lay down there in a crumpled position, softly cursing. As I watched, he came to his knees, crawled to a bunk, pulled himself up and sat there with his head in his hands, his elbows resting on his knees.

I went down and looked at him. Just stood and

looked at him.

He couldn't keep his elbows balanced on his knees. They wobbled and slipped off. He would carefully place them back each time. They would slip, and his head jerked down. He gave that up. He sat there, hanging out over the bunk like the broken limb of a once-sturdy tree.

"Have it out with whom?" I said.

"Whom-diddy-whom-whom — whom — *whom!*" he said. "Bull-crap," he said. He smiled unhappily at the deck.

"Have it out with whom?" I said.

"Bull-crap," he said. "Ivor vanished," he said. "Can't see me for dust, anyway, no-how. Not really. Love her. Love two women. How you love two women? Sisters. One a whore and the other a — " He ceased.

"A what?"

"A lovely. A love. She gone anyway. 'Oh, Elk,' she say. 'You are just a darling big old bear.' She said that and I 'dore her, the ground she walks on — all that crap. Love wife, too."

"You're getting pretty wild. Maybe you need a drink."

"Prolly so."

"I just came from your house," I said. "As I was leaving, a gray forty-nine Ford sedan drove up. Had a missing hubcap on the right front wheel. Anybody you know drive a car like that?"

"Sure."

"Who?"

"Me."

Maybe I was too tired. I stared at him. I felt crazier than usual.

"You sure it might be your car?"

"Positive," he said. "It *is* my car. Couldn't be anybody else's car but mine. How many gray forty-nine Fords have missing hubcaps right front wheel?" He waved his hand and nearly fell off the bunk. "If came to my home, then's mine car. Isn't that logical?"

"Anything could be logical right now," I said. "Who drives it mostly?"

"Me. I drive it mostly. In fact, nobody else but me drives it. I keep it over at Vine Tree, use it as a fishing boat, I mean, fishing car. You know, lakes and rivers, rivers and lakes. Like to fish. By God, I think I'll go fishing. Whyn't you come fishing with me? We could...."

I said loudly, "Shut up!" I was nervous. I could hardly control my voice. I said as quietly as I could, "What's this Vine Tree you mentioned?" I could remember Ivor Hendrix saying those words over the phone on this boat. Now he was saying them. She'd denied the words.

"My other place," he said. "North side town. Call it Vine Tree, because there's a big old tree with a vine hanging on it." He started to laugh, belched instead. "Stomach burns," he said. "Not eat enough. Reason."

"Did you talk with Ivor on the phone this morning, when she was here on your boat?"

"Nah. She wouldn't talk with me. I let her be."

"Did you talk with her this morning? Try and remember. Did you talk with her and maybe mention Vine Tree?"

"No. Never, not me. Memory like elephant."

She had told me she'd been talking with Elk.

"Listen," I said. "Did you go down to see her at the Vista Groves Hotel? Where I told you she was?"

"No. Was — but I got drunk instead."

"Did you tell anybody where she was?"

"Don't think so. You asked me not to."

"But did you maybe tell somebody?"

"Don't think so." He shrugged. "Might've."

I was mad as hell now. The son-of-a-bitch sat there grinning and reeling and belching on the bunk.

"She's gone," I said. I said it very carefully. "She was taken away. By force." I tried to play on this great goddamned love of his that he claimed he had for her. "The room was wrecked."

He came reeling to his feet, lurched around, plowed into me, and fell down. He crawled around, then got back on the bunk and sat.

"Who did you tell?" I said.

I thought he would cry. "I don't know. Honest, God."

"Where's Vine Tree?"

He gave me the address in the north side of town.

I said, "Try to remember if you told somebody about where she was. Try, for hell's sake!"

He lurched to his feet and stood as solid as a tree. He shouted, "How do I know? I don't know. Leave me alone, God damn it I can't be trusted when I drink. The hell with it." He turned and crashed to the other side of the cabin. He clawed into a cupboard and came out with a bottle of whisky. He turned to me, digging at the tape around the cap of the bottle.

"Get to hell off my boat. Insult me, you bastard. Go! I'm going sail Mexico today. Go fish off banks."

I watched him. Tears welled thickly in his eyes. He tore the tape off the bottle and fumbled with the cap. He got that off. It rattled on the deck. He guzzled from the bottle. Whisky streamed down his chest and splashed on his feet.

He shouted, "Sail Mexico!"

I shouted back at him. *"Bon voyage!"*

I got out of there. As I reached the lawn at the end of the pier, I paused and looked back. Elk Crafford was reeling around on the pier, untying lines and heaving them at the *Carol*. He leaped up the gangplank. The schooner eased away from the pier on a swell. The gangplank gave way. He caught the rail, slung himself up onto the deck.

I turned for my car, stopped, then ran in a long diagonal, off across the yacht club lawn. A police cruiser nosed into the parking area. Probably this was a regular check-point for me. I cut out around the clubhouse, climbed a wire fence, ran through bushes to the yellow Dodge. I had parked it outside in the street.

I was scared now, and I didn't like it.

I made the car, and drove off toward the north side of town.

TWENTY-SIX

Vine Tree. The words were painted in white on an un-barked slab of oak. The small sign was mounted on a brass post.

I stopped the car. It was one of the oldest and wealthiest residential sections in the city. This particular lot must have encompassed ten acres. A fifteen-foot-high whitewashed cement wall, covered with shocks of green vine, slanted from partially opened mahogany gates. The gates had large black wrought-iron hinges and locks. It had probably been a beautiful estate back around twenty-five or six. It was pretty well run down.

I reached back and patted the hound, told him to stay put. He cracked a couple of yaks, wrinkled his snout, and went back to snoozing. I got out of the car and walked to the gate.

Beyond a meandering drive inside, I saw the house, rising through trees against a gray witch's sky. It was like something off an old Gothic postcard.

Fresh tire marks showed in the worn gravel drive.

Probably this was the old Crafford estate. Elk had gone through the family inheritance, held on to this but had been unable to keep it up.

I moved fast, walking through the gate. I passed ancient gardens and marble pools, rock gardens, sundials, and tall urns containing sear, withered ferns. Oak, fresh saplings, straight hickorys, and uncared-for fruit trees; orange, key lime, grapefruit and wild cherry grew thickly. Willows leaned like pale dead hands above empty pools. Rain drove with winds across the treetops.

I heard the scream. It lifted, roofing the afternoon.

I ran toward the house.

Again the scream sliced through the chill rain. It hurt to hear it. It was a woman in pain.

I was still some distance from the house. It was surrounded by a thick clotting of shrubs and trees. It gutted toward the raining sky in a thrust of cupolas, windows, spires, and furious gingerbread. It was graced with two-foot black beams and the long, graceful galleries of the southland. Guest houses were set away from the main house. It was winged and multiroomed, immense and once-grand.

The scream again, more a throbbing yell of terror.

Then silence. I reached the house, swung up on a gallery railing and went to the house wall beside a tall window. I felt dwarfed. The windows were draped.

Feet pounded from up above. There was the sound of a falling body, and a short feminine cry.

I moved fast. Toward the rear, a door swung to and fro in the steady wind. I went inside, hearing the sound of my own breathing. The house was darkly shadowed, heavy with gleaming sienna woodwork.

I moved past back stairs. I heard voices and walked as softly as I could through large rooms of gloom, past ghostly furniture covered with dusty sheets.

"Don't try it again," a man said.

I stopped, my heart yammering. The voice went on speaking. It echoed from distance. I had a crazed sensation of not being where I was. I had no gun. I knew this was the end of the road. I knew the answers now — always too late. Yet even with what she had done, I was frightened for her. I couldn't help myself.

"You'd better tell us now," the man said. "You know you'll tell us."

I had never heard that voice.

A woman laughed, said, "Let Stewart," and I heard the sound of flesh striking flesh.

A stairway led upward. I took it. It sloped in a steep spiral. Gold-framed mirrors clung to an octagonal wall. The stairwell ascended straight up like a vertical tunnel. It was a vicious climb leading to a skylight where rain slashed thick water-green glass. The light down the stairwell was ghastly, my hands and clothes a sickly green.

The man grunted. He said, "Now." There was something bright and mean in the voice. The scream was short and sharp. It pealed through the house. I came onto a landing, moved toward a partially open doorway and stood against the wall.

"She's got to tell us, Carl," Asa Crafford said. "She'll tell us if you'll just hurt her enough. She never could stand to be hurt much. We can't hang around here forever."

I saw them. I began to go nuts.

"I'll tell you nothing," Ivor Hendrix said. The words were bitter and painful. There was pain in the sound of her voice, but there was strength, too. "You can all go to hell. You can kill me, I won't tell you." She breathed heavily as she spoke.

She was stretched over the rail at the foot of a large bedstead in a grotesque, bone-wrenching position. Her arms were tied with rope to the rail. Her body hung of its own weight to the floor, knees bent, her head flung back. She watched them dreamily through the slanted eyes. Her red mouth was touched with disdain. She was completely naked.

A man I had never seen hulked above her.

He said, "Look, Ivor," with a kind of tight patience. "You think I enjoy this? Can't you understand you've got to tell me? You will sooner or later. There's no choice."

She cursed him tiredly.

"Oh, for Christ's sake," Asa Crafford said. "*Make* her talk. You're too easy on her. Let Stewart...."

"You just close your flap," the man said. "You have too much to say." The man was Carl Hendrix. I remembered him from the snapshots. The slightly popped eyes, the sober expression. He was stockier than I recalled from the photos. He wore a pale blue tropical worsted suit, a white shirt open at the collar, and no tie. He looked at Ivor, gnawed his lower lip, then rubbed his eyes as if in mental pain. He seemed undecisive.

Asa Crafford said in a whisper that was harsh and intense, "Let Stewart!"

Another man spoke. I couldn't see him. It was watermelon-puss, all right. "Quit saying that," he said. "I'm hired to work for you. I haven't been paid as yet. You're crazy," he said. "Both of you. You're gone too far and you know it." He said more quietly, "Jesus Christ — do something, but get it over with."

Asa Crafford said, "He wants his money, but he has a weak stomach. Isn't that comical? A killer — a paid killer, with a weak stomach?"

Carl Hendrix turned fast and struck Asa Crafford across the face. It was a hard blow. She stumbled back out of sight.

"You crazy bitch!" Carl Hendrix said. He turned back to Ivor, and stared down at her. "Look," he said. "We know you got onto this thing. I know you swiped the money. You think I'm stupid?"

"Yes," Ivor Hendrix said. "I think you're stupid."

He held his patience with obvious effort. Nobody said anything for a moment. The house was silent with only the sound of distant rain.

"What did you tell that fool dick?" Hendrix said.

Ivor said nothing. Her clothes were in a pile beside the bed.

Hendrix said, "Honey, you're in this just as much as we are. You've done it all yourself. It's a lot of money. Enough for everybody." He leaned down and shouted at her, "Why don't you tell me where it is!"

He took hold of her, shaking her. She stared at him. He slammed his hand back and forth across her face. She held her head up and spat at him. She spat again. He looked shocked. His face choked with rage. He cursed her, and struck her savagely in the belly with his fist.

I lost my head.

As I headed into the room, he swung again, striking his fist against the girl's unprotected middle. He grunted and she yelled, then gasped breathlessly.

"Tell me!" he shouted.

Asa Crafford saw me. I shoved her out of the way and dove at Carl Hendrix. He turned, his eyes a little gone with what he was doing. I hit him with everything I had. He yelled something. I caught the front of his shirt and yanked so hard it shredded in my hand. I smashed him, and felt the bone of my fist against the bone of his face. My cracked knuckle bled white pain to my elbow. I wanted to kill him. He kicked for my groin. I grabbed his foot, put my shoulder into it, and whipped him to the floor. I leaped on him. He rolled and grabbed for my face, his fingers raking my jaw.

I got my hands on his throat, knelt on his shoulders,

and slammed his head against the floor. I wanted to smash his skull on the flowered carpet.

A gun exploded. The carpet spat dust close to Hendrix's head.

"You fool!" Asa Crafford said.

"Get off him," the man called Stewart said.

I rolled off and looked up.

The ugly face looked down at me. He was pale and grim, with the .45 in his fist.

"Take it slow," he said. "Get on your feet."

I stood up. Ivor Hendrix moaned from the bed.

I heard a telephone ring downstairs.

"Never mind that," Asa Crafford said.

I looked over at Ivor Hendrix. She stared at me as if she had never seen me before. A thin hair of blood appeared at the corner of her mouth. She lowered her eyes.

TWENTY-SEVEN

Carl Hendrix sat up on the floor. He touched his fingers to his nose. They came away painted bright red. He brought out a handkerchief and gently blew his nose, dabbing at the blood. He stood up and faced me.

His eyes were dull above the red handkerchief.

"What now?" the man with the gun said.

Carl Hendrix took the handkerchief away from his nose.

He said, "What do you suppose? It's obvious, isn't it? We'll continue just as we were doing." He looked at me and frowned, then looked at Stewart. "I told you to watch Baron every minute. You didn't do much of a job. You haven't done much of a job from the beginning."

Stewart was a mountain of a man. The head and face seemed much more grotesque than the night I'd first met him. He wore a belted trench coat that was soaking wet, and a soft felt hat. He looked strangely sad. It was not an expression of the moment.

Stewart said, "This isn't a job. It's a fouled-up mess, Hendrix. I've stuck because I need the money. I'm going to get the money if I have to operate on that one — " he nodded toward Ivor — "myself. I mean it."

"Where were you before you came in?" Hendrix said to Stewart.

"I went to the house, looking for Elk. He wasn't there. Then I tried the boat. The *Carol's* gone. I think I saw it out in the bay. Looked like him hanging over the rail out there."

Asa Crafford was watching me. She had on a pair of skin-tight black toreador pants, drawn with white thread at the calves. She wore a white blouse and a thin off-red cashmere sweater. She had yellow moccasins on her feet. Her black hair was heavy on the left side. She didn't seem to fit into this gathering. I knew she belonged solidly.

"Poor Elk," she said. "He's such a fool."

Steward said, "So I came back here."

I said, "He should have been at the *Carol* before I was. I talked with Elk at the pier. I saw Stewart leave the house. Maybe he's crossing you, Hendrix."

Stewart said, "I beat you here, didn't I? I stopped for

a drink." He looked at me. "You're loaded with ideas, aren't you," he said.

"How did you get into the house before I did?"

"I came the front way. You must've taken the back." He paused, looking around the room, holding the gun loosely. "I'm sick of you people. You make me want to vomit. But I still want my money."

The phone rang again downstairs.

"Ten to one it's Elk," Asa said. "When he's drunk on his boat, he keeps calling ship-to-shore through the Tampa marine operator. He takes the *Carol* out into the Gulf, then keeps phoning, checking on me. It's rich."

I said, "The law is on the phone. You think I'd come here, knowing what I know, without posting them?"

"He's lying," Stewart said. "The law would enjoy slitting his throat."

"Baron?" Carl Hendrix said through the red handkerchief. "How much of this do you know about?"

"Everything," I said. I went over and began unfastening the ropes on Ivor Hendrix's arms. She did not look at me.

"Let him untie her," Carl Hendrix said. "I think maybe we'd better get out of here, anyway. Go someplace in the country."

I finished untying Ivor's arms. She slumped to the floor, looked up at me. She did not smile. Maybe she wanted to smile. She was badly hurt. The pain was in her eyes. She came to one knee and said, "Thanks, Lee."

"Get dressed," I said. "Hurry up."

"He's giving orders, now," Stewart said.

"Don't you like looking at her?" Asa said. "I think she has a beautiful body. A little top-heavy, but aside from that — " She stepped over by me. Ivor Hendrix went to her clothes and began dressing. She moved painfully, her lower lip between her teeth. Asa Crafford said, "How much do you really know, Lee?"

I looked at her. She smiled with her teeth. There was nothing in her eyes at all. A strange woman.

I said, "Everything I need to know."

Stewart was watching Ivor dress. There was small lust in his eyes. He watched her closely, his eyes moving up and down her body in a kind of deliberate caress. I didn't like the way he looked at her. I couldn't get how I felt about her out of my head.

Stewart would kill me. I knew that. They would kill me first, probably. They might kill me before they left here, because there was no reason for my going along with them. If they went.

Asa Crafford said, "Would you like a crack at that, Stewart? Why don't you go ahead?"

Hendrix grunted. He threw the handkerchief to the floor. His nose had ceased bleeding, but the upper lip and the area around his nose was covered with blood. He went over to Ivor. She had the sheath dress on, and was trying to button it up across her breasts. He tore her hands away, grabbed her by the hair, and struck her four times across the face. He grunted with each slap.

He shouted, "Where's the money!"

She lay back on the bed and said. "Go to hell." She wasn't crying, but there were tears in her eyes.

There was only one way out. That might not work.

It probably wouldn't help any. But it might stop them.

"Stewart?" Hendrix said, stepping back from where Ivor lay on the bed. "It's up to you. I want to know where she's got the money. Find out."

Stewart came slowly across the room. Handing his gun to Hendrix, he said, "Hold them." He went over to Ivor Hendrix and looked at her and grinned. It was the god-damndest grin I'd ever seen; the misshapen face and the enormous hulk of man. He said, "Honey, you want to tell them? Or you want me to do something to you. I can make you talk, you know? Which is it?"

She stared up at him. She seemed to cringe faintly on the bed, her lips parted.

"All right," he said. He didn't move. "Take your pants off again, honey. I'm going to do something to you. Come on, hurry up."

She didn't move. She seemed frozen in her position on the bed. She didn't blink. She didn't even seem to breathe.

"All right," Stewart said. He reached down and pulled her dress up to her waist. She wore tight black briefs. He leaned above her and something queer crossed his face; an expression of sad and breathless patience. He ran one hand up her thigh, staring. The hand was trembling and I knew the reasons he'd given for not pursuing his medical career were figments of a wild imagination. His lips seemed to bubble faintly, and he reached out, snarled his fingers in the waist of the briefs and began peeling them down.

"Wait," I heard myself say. "Hold on. I think I can help you — if you'll tell me a couple of things."

Stewart didn't seem to hear me. He went on slowly drawing Ivor Hendrix's pants off.

"Wait, God damn it," I said. I looked at Carl Hendrix. Hendrix looked fascinated. I moved fast and grabbed Stewart's shoulder, whirled him around. He breathed heavily. His eyes were glazed, unseeing. Then they slowly cleared.

"Why did you stop me?" he said. He spoke softly.

"You slimy bastard," I said.

He stared at me. Ivor Hendrix pulled her dress down and lay silently on the bed.

Hendrix said, "If you know something, Baron, let's hear it. Otherwise — " He left the sentence unfinished.

"Yes," Asa Crafford said. "How can you help, Lee?" She said it to me, but she was watching Stewart with round, wide eyes. Then she looked at me.

I said, "I know where the money is." I jerked my head at Ivor. "She may *think* she knows. But she doesn't. I do know."

Asa's voice was excited. "He's telling the truth. I can tell."

I said, "But I'm bargaining. It won't do you any good to try and make me tell you. I've stood up against worse than you've got here, including the big boy, and I do mean boy. I want to know a few things first."

Hendrix frowned. "You're in no position to bargain. What good will it do?"

"What harm will it do?" I said.

I watched them all. Time was the one element I had to have. I was playing for it. My shirt was plastered to my body with sweat.

I said, "I'm curious. I've been working hard. I'd like

to know some answers."

"I thought you knew everything," Asa said.

Ivor Hendrix stared at me, puzzled. A dim light of greed showed in her eyes.

"All right," Carl Hendrix said. "What you want to know?"

I went over to Ivor. "Yonkers was the man who came to see your husband. He had already killed his partner, Horace Ailings. Right?" She nodded, watching me, still puzzled. I said, "How did you learn about the robbery — the money? Go ahead," I said. "Tell me. Believe me, it doesn't make any difference any more."

She half sat up, then sat up all the way. Her eyes were startled. "I heard them," she said. "That's what they were fighting about. Carl found out Yonkers had the money and Yonkers hid it. I saw him hide it — he buried it. He was afraid Carl would take it from him, because he was very sick."

"You bitch," Carl Hendrix said.

She didn't bother looking his way. "Carl kept asking me to take a trip — go away. He finally got me to agree to visit his aunt in Orlando. He figured with me away, he could *make* Yonkers talk. He knew the man was dying. Yonkers had told him he'd give him some of the money, but Carl wanted it all." She shrugged. "I was sick of it. Sick of how he'd let Elk take all our money and shoot it away. Sick of how he sat around! I dug up the money and went away. The fool." She looked at her husband. "He starved Yonkers — tortured him. Yonkers told him the truth, where he'd hidden the money. But Carl only found the empty suitcase. He didn't believe Yonkers was telling him the truth. The operation Yonkers had was infected, so he just died. It must have sent Carl crazy."

"Where's the money now!" Hendrix said.

"Don't tell him," I said. "He agreed to a bargain. Besides," I said. "You don't know where it is now, Ivor." I turned to Hendrix. "You weren't working alone," I said. "You and Asa were together on the thing, weren't you?"

Asa Crafford shrugged. "I did all I could to keep you tied up, honey — didn't you like it?"

Stewart interrupted. "This is getting us no place. What the hell you bothering with him for?"

"Just shut up," Hendrix said.

I said, "Only all the time there was a guy named Vince Gamba. He'd been snooping around and he knew plenty. He was scared for Ivor. There was no greed in him. He was in love with her. He didn't know where she was. He was going through hell. He found Yonkers' body, hacked up like that."

Hendrix said, "It was her idea," looking at Asa. "She wanted to cut him up and distribute the pieces. We couldn't do it. We eliminated the fingerprint angle, his face — " He ceased talking, remembering and not liking what he remembered.

"You'll never get that dough now, Hendrix," I said.

"You know where it is?"

"Yeah."

"We'll get it."

"You're God-damned right we'll get it," Stewart said. He went over and took his gun from Hendrix and faced me. "You ever been shot in the kneecaps?" he said. He was healthy again. A real hot shot. I ignored him.

I looked at Ivor. "You killed Vince Gamba," I said. "Too bad. A mistake. I should never have told you he called me, saying he wanted to tell me where the money was. He only thought he knew. He buried Yonkers' body, hiding it so you wouldn't be hurt. He was right when he figured the cops would eventually get to you and you would break. You went to his place, planning to kill him — maybe with that .32 automatic. You must have got that from around the trailer, where Yonkers left it. Gamba was passed out drunk. You fixed him in the oven, turned on the gas and left the gun to implicate him. You planted that letter on him so it'd look like suicide for love. You must have seen the letter he started writing to you. That could be misinterpreted, too. But not if you thought about it. He was referring to the money and what he knew you'd done — not to his love."

Hendrix said, "I knew she was laying for him." He looked at her. "How long, bitch?"

"Weeks and weeks," she said. "So what?"

I said, "Then you beat it in Gamba's station wagon, got a bottle and soused yourself up, and came back and found me there. You knew I'd be there. It would be perfect. It nearly was."

"I never thought she had it in her," Asa said.

"Gamba had discovered where the arms were buried, and he buried the body with them. He went around carefully destroying evidence. That fouled me up with the police." I stared at Ivor. "He did all that to help you, honey. And you killed him for it. Nice, isn't it?"

She turned her face away.

I looked at Hendrix. "You knew when I began to move in. You'd already hired Stewart to keep watch on the trailer, for your wife. He saw me. You know why she hired me? So I could find you before you found her. The cops would believe she was straight, maybe. Even if they didn't, she would still have the money after it was all over. She'd done nothing wrong, if she kept shut — until she murdered Gamba." I paused. "But if you could find her first, you figured you'd make her talk. Like now. You've found how hard that is. I don't think happy boy here could either."

"We're wasting time," Hendrix said.

"She doesn't know where the money is any more," I said. I looked at her. "Poor Gamba," I said. "He's the guy who answered the phone at the trailer when I called the first time. All he was thinking about was you."

"Shut up!" she yelled. "Can't you shut up!"

"The dick's lying," Stewart said. "He just wanted to make sure of things. He doesn't know where the money is. I'm going to find out."

He moved fast over to Ivor and looked down at her. "This time, honey," he said. "You get it — whether you like it or not." He reached for her.

She grabbed his wrist and sank her teeth into it. Blood spurted. He bellowed and drew back his arm to strike her with the gun in his fist. I knew he might kill her.

"Wait!" I shouted.

He paused, his eyes wild.

I took the bank books out of my pocket and threw them on the floor. They bounced.

"There's the money," I said. "Fight over it."

Ivor Hendrix's eyes were large and full of fright. She leaped off the bed. She knew what was going to happen. She ran hard for the bedroom door.

Stewart's expression was still touched with the anger of a moment before. He lifted the .45 and shot her in the back as she ran into the hall.

My heart stopped at the sound of that gun.

The slug caught her in the middle of the spine. He fired again, standing there, his face pale. You knew her back was broken. She arched the wrong way. She fell down and did not move.

There was the pungent odor of burned cordite in the room. There was silence.

I turned to Hendrix. "Her blood is on you," I said. "On you — get that."

He stared at me.

"Look at those bank books," I said. "She'd have to sign them. She'll never sign them now."

Stewart stood in the strained pose with the gun still pointed at the doorway. I knew he was ready to kill anybody. He was confused.

Hendrix was looking at the bank books. He dropped them and moved toward Stewart with the stance of a maniac. The gun in Stewart's fist turned and pointed at Hendrix.

"Don't," Stewart said.

I bulled at Hendrix's back. Stewart turned the gun barrel and fired at me without changing expression. My left shoulder was smashed. I whirled, trying to stay on my feet. The gun roared again. I went at Stewart and caught his ankles and yanked. He came down hard. I heard the noises I was making. I kept hitting him, smashing at his face with everything in me. There was no pain in my shoulder right then. I was insensible to pain.

Hendrix tried to pull me off Stewart. It only made it worse. I kneed the man, and he screamed. I did it again and he screamed again. I got hold of his gun hand. It was limp. I grabbed the gun, thrust my foot into his gut, and turned on Hendrix and Asa.

"I'll kill you if you move," I said.

I stood up and walked out into the hall. Stewart groaned in a huddle by the bed. He hugged his groin, his eyes rolled back into his skull. I wondered hopefully if I had maimed him for life.

Ivor Hendrix lay on the floor in the hall. She was alive. I didn't touch her.

"Come on, you two." I herded Asa and Carl Hendrix downstairs and called the police. I talked with Lowell Haddock and asked him to send an ambulance to this address as quickly as possible.

Then we went back upstairs. Nobody spoke. Stewart hadn't moved.

I knelt beside Ivor Hendrix and held her head. I tried to make her as comfortable as possible. I kept the gun handy.

Asa and Carl Hendrix stood in the bedroom and argued for a time. She cried bitterly. She cursed him. He finally stood with a strange, numb expression on his face. He had picked up the bank books. He held them in both hands as if they were alive, and stared at them that way.

There was nothing I could do for Ivor Hendrix. She

did not speak. I didn't think she felt any pain. She kept watching me silently. The truth is, she didn't really see me — she saw nothing.

I watched her die. After a while, she was dead, lying in my arms. There was something that I'd almost had, but that I would never have now. What she had done wouldn't have mattered. Nothing would have mattered where she was concerned.

You can't go back to that first dream. Don't try.

I laid her down carefully. Then I quit looking at her, stood up, and walked into the bedroom.

"We may as well go downstairs," I said. "They'll be along soon."

TWENTY-EIGHT

I went in to see Chief of Homicide Lowell Haddock the next morning. He looked tired, sitting there behind his desk. He had dark gray hair and a heavy, meaty face that was dark red, probably because of high blood pressure. His eyes were brown and small and intelligent. The whites of his eyes were muddy because he seldom got enough sleep. He tried hard to do his job well.

He sat there looking at me, with a dead, well chewed cigar in the brass ash tray on the desk. Sweat streamed down the sides of his face.

"There'll be a one year's revocation of license," he said. He continued to watch me. "Maybe I'm sorry about that. If I am sorry, it's because of old Jim."

I said nothing.

He said, "I'd get my ass et if I didn't put it before the board. You had it coming."

I moved to a more comfortable position in the stiff-backed chair facing his desk, tendering my left arm in the sling. I said, "Maybe I have, at that."

Sweat dangled on his upper lip. He blew it off and smeared his face with one hand.

"Cocky," he said. "Cocky, and with a lot to learn."

I didn't speak.

"How's the shoulder?" he said.

"Kind of stiff. Doc Hestern gave me a needle about two hours ago. It's holding. He dressed it fine."

Watching me, he looked angered. He blew some sweat off, reached under his desk and came up with a dirty towel. He mopped his face, then threw the towel back under the desk. Behind him, the alley window was open. The sun in the alley was very bright.

"Get any sleep?" he said.

"Your beds aren't so hot," I said. "I feel like a waffle iron. I'll sleep tonight, I guess. I don't seem to feel tired."

"I suppose you think I'm a son-of-a-bitch and all that — getting your license revoked, raising hell with you the way I did when they brought you in last night."

"It's all right. I was a little mad, then. I'm okay now."

He turned his gaze down as if it was the hardest thing the world to do and stared at the blotter on his desk, reached for his cigar, but didn't touch it.

"So," he said. "You were a little mad, but it's all okay now." He paused, still staring at the blotter. When he looked up at me, his eyes were plain angry. "You really honest-to-God expect to keep working in this town?"

"Yeah."

"Using Jim's old office?"

"Uh-huh."

"Jim and I were good friends."

"So I hear."

He smeared the sweat around on his face.

"You've got a hell of a lot more to learn than I figured," he said.

"Some of the boys you employ have a lot to learn."

He sighed deeply. "Maybe I should've let them go ahead and press charges against you. It took some damned fast talking to calm those *boys* you're speaking of."

"Okay," I said. "Is that all?"

"No, it damned well isn't all, my friend." He leaned forward on his desk, staring at me. "You talk about your old man being a nothing — a phony...."

"I didn't say that."

"And I didn't like hearing it. But I'll tell you this. You'll really have to be a hot baby to keep working in this town. Because, for you, Lee, it's going to be a very, very hot town."

"I like them hot."

He stared at me, blinked slowly, and sat back. His voice changed, became more businesslike. "There was a reward," he said. "Of course, you knew about that."

"Yes. Sure."

"Well, for old Jim's sake, I'm getting you off the griddle using your share of the money to pay up a couple of citizens who are slightly bothered."

"Who's that?"

He spoke softly. "A guy who runs a gas station. Name

of Bronsky. Seems you stole his car and fouled it up. I saw the interior. It looks like an army camped in the back seat." He paused. "Then there's a small matter of a stolen boat."

"Okay."

"Okay, the man says. Okay!" He snapped his finger "Just like that, it's all okay. What about all the rest of it? You have generally mucked up. Don't you realize that?"

"I realize it."

"You withheld evidence. You beat up two of my men. You played hell with them. Rudy Vagas and Lew Steifer. All right, I calmed them a little. But they won't change toward you. And they'll probably be around a long time."

I didn't say anything.

"Sad, isn't it," he said. "Sad, hell. Well," he said. "You might be interested in this. We had the Tampa marine operator put out a call to all ships to watch for that drunk — Elk Crafford. A shrimper spotted him about nine-thirty this morning. Said it was the *Carol*, all right. About forty miles off Nokomis. Riding out a calm, under full sail. They took a close look. He was drunk as hell, wandering around on deck, swearing at the seagulls. A Coast Guard launch went out to pick him up."

"Well," I said. I stood up. The arm was aching a little. That was all.

"What you going to do for a year?" he said.

"First I'll finish cleaning up the office," I said. "Then maybe just take it easy, get to know this country again."

He grunted and sat there. "Yeah," he said. "You could damned well afford to do that, all right." He paused, then said, "We found the station wagon. This Gamba's. There was one woman's shoe in it, caught up under the front seat."

"It figures," I said.

"You stood in the way of police procedure, Lee."

There was nothing I could say.

"Your old man," he said. "He didn't work the way you want to work."

I shrugged.

"You think it won't be tough?" he said. "It's going to be goddamned tough."

I shrugged again.

He had about run out. There was a lot more he wanted to say, but he wouldn't say it.

"It's a bitch of a thing," he said. "This business. All that killing. No damned excuse."

"Yeah," I said. "I'll see you, Lowell."

He nodded. "Lee?" he said as I reached the door. "There's a slim chance I might be able to work it for six months, instead of a year."

We looked at each other. "Don't do it if it's going to break your heart," I said.

He just stared at me.

"But," I said. "I'd appreciate it."

"Go on," he said. "The hell with you."

I went outside into the corridor and closed the door. Two plainclothes men were talking over by the drinking fountain. They looked at me and went into a huddle. A sharply dressed blonde walked swiftly out of Missing Persons with a sheaf of papers in her hand.

She started upstairs, her heels smacking.

I walked down the corridor and saw the hound sitting there. My hound, now. I wondered what I would call him. He was a black shadow against the sunlight. He lifted his behind, gaped at me, and we moved down into the street together. It was hot and the traffic was heavy. I blinked against the sunshine.

We passed a corner phone booth. I remembered something, and told the hound to wait. He plunked himself down. I went inside the booth and looked up the number of another girl I had loved madly once. As I dialed the number I wondered if she had ever married, or if she were still loving free lance. I wondered if she had a dog, so we could double-date. I wondered if she had any corpses she'd like investigated.

I almost hung up. Almost, but not quite.

Life must go on.

THE END

Gil Brewer was born Nov. 20, 1922 in Canandaigua, NY. After leaving the army at the end of WWII, he joined his family who had settled in St. Petersburg, Florida. There he met Verlaine in 1947 and married her soon after. Brewer started by writing serious novels, but soon turned to paperback originals after a sale to Gold Medal Books in 1950. At his height, he was a brilliant writer

of sharply defined noir thrillers, usually involving a male protagonist driven to crime by the sexual allure of a young siren. But unwilling to promote himself, his career took a turn for the worse after a mental breakdown, and a long decline into alcoholism. Brewer died on Jan. 9, 1983.

GIL BREWER BIBLIOGRAPHY

NOVELS:

Love Me and Die (1951; w/Day Keene, published as by Day Keene)
Satan is a Woman (1951)
So Rich, So Dead (1951)
13 French Street (1951)
Flight to Darkness (1952)
Hell's Our Destination (1953)
A Killer is Loose (1954)
Some Must Die (1954)
77 Rue Paradis (1954)
The Squeeze (1955)
The Red Scarf (1955)
—And the Girl Screamed (1956)
The Angry Dream (1957; reprinted as *The Girl from Hateville*, 1958)
The Brat (1957)
Little Tramp (1958)
The Bitch (1958)
Wild (1958)
The Vengeful Virgin (1958)
Sugar (1959)
Wild to Possess (1959)
Angel (1960)
Nude on Thin Ice (1960)
Backwoods Teaser (1960)
The Three-Way Split (1960)
Play it Hard (1960)
Appointment in Hell (1961)
A Taste for Sin (1961)
Memory of Passion (1962)
The Hungry One (1966)
The Tease (1967)
Sin for Me (1967)
It Takes a Thief #1: The Devil in Davos (1969)
It Takes a Thief #2: Mediterranean Caper (1969)
It Takes a Thief #3: Appointment in Cairo (1970)
A Devil for O'Shaugnessy (2008)
The Erotics (2015)
Gun the Dame Down (2015)
Angry Arnold (2015)

As Harry Arvay

Eleven Bullets for Mohammed (1975)
Operation Kuwait (1975)
The Moscow Intercept (1975)
The Piraeus Plot (1975)
Togo Commando (1976)

As Mark Bailey

Mouth Magic (1972)

As Al Conroy
Soldato #3: Strangle Hold!
  (1973)
Soldato #4: Murder
  Mission! (1973)

As Hal Ellson
Blood on the Ivy (1970)

As Elaine Evans
Shadowland (1970)
A Dark and Deadly Love
  (1972)
Black Autumn (1973)
Wintershade (1974)

As Luke Morgann
More Than a Handful
  (1972)
Ladies in Heat (1972)
Gamecock (1972)
Tongue Tricks! (1972)

As Ellery Queen
The Campus Murders
  (1969)
The Japanese Golden
  Dozen (1978; rewrites by
  Brewer)

STORY COLLECTIONS:

Redheads Die Quickly and
  Other Stories (2012,
  revised 2019; edited by
  David Rachels)
Death is a Private Eye:
  Unpublished Stories
  (2019; edited by David
  Rachels)
Die Once—Die Twice: More
  Unpublished Stories
  (2020; edited by David
  Rachels)
Death Comes Last: The
  Rest of the 1950s (2021;
  edited by David Rachels)

**UNPUBLISHED
NOVELS**

House of the Potato
  (autobiographical novel,
  late 1940s)
Firebase Seattle
  (Executioner novel, 1975)
The Paper Coffin (spy
  novel, 1970s)

9 7 9 8 8 8 6 0 1 1 0 9 8